AFTER DARKNESS FALLS

AFTER DARKNESS FALLS, BOOK ONE

After Darkness Falls
(After Darkness Falls #1)
May Sage
Cover by Clarissa Yeo of Yocla Designs
Photography by Lindee Robinson
Edited by Cara Quinlan
Proofread by Theresa Schultz

CONTENTS

To my brother-in-law, Antoine, and my sister, Eva, who are fighting a battle with the bravery of warriors.

Eastbound

CHAPTER

1

Just because a piece of advice was given by a serial killer didn't necessarily mean that it was wrong.

Chloe's father used to say, "If your day sucks, concentrate on one thing you can look forward to, and you'll get through it." At the time, she hadn't known that he'd been distracting himself from his dreary routine by imagining what torture he'd administer to the victims he kept locked in the storm cellar, but still. Great advice.

She put it into practice, trying to forget why she was on a plane for the first time in her life and focusing on new experiences, and the destination. She managed a smile. Seven years ago, she might have even broken into a victory dance. Now, at twenty-five, after working her ass off night and day to pay the bills, a smile was all she had.

She'd changed. Not all of it was for the worse. Chloe was mature enough to recognize that she'd been self-centered in her teens; otherwise, she would have noted the strange things—the smells, the disappearances, the odd noises that didn't quite sound like they'd come from a TV. But she'd been too busy studying in her room, music blasting in her earphones, to care about what her father was doing.

Her world imploded in so many ways. With a father arrested, and then convicted as a serial killer, she never had a chance. The colleges that had shown some interest in her were all quick to dispatch rejection letters. None of her personal achievements had mattered in the end. Grades, chess, track, debate clubs—all had been for naught. She was George Miller's daughter, and that was that. The name stuck to her skin like a bad scent.

Her brother disappeared that same year. She couldn't really blame him. She also would have poofed into thin air, if she'd known how. Instead, Chloe had to grow up fast. She sold the house, sending all the profits to the victims' families to pay for their funerals and everything else they had to deal with in the aftermath. That hadn't stopped them from sending insults and threats, but they kept the money, and hopefully it helped. Then, Chloe left Colorado with her beat-up Beetle, her old cat, and a backpack in the trunk. Fast-forward seven years, and she was doing okay.

But *okay* had never been her aspiration.

Chloe soon found out that some people were more understanding than others. While humans—regular humans like her—weren't entirely welcoming to the daughter of a cannibalistic murderer, sups didn't seem to care.

Since the Age of Blood, when the supernaturals had announced their existence to the world, they'd mostly kept to themselves, living in gated, tight-knit communities, but occasionally, someone who didn't fit in joined the regular human world. In her travels, Chloe met some shifters, mostly loners. They were a little unsettling at first, but she soon started to seek them out purposely. She preferred their company to the judgmental people who blamed her for someone else's sins. Sups entirely shrugged off her history.

They all had a horrific story about an uncle, cousin, or sister who'd gone rogue. Among sups, all that mattered was your own actions.

"One of my brothers went feral. He tried to eat my da'. We hunted him down, though."

Some people said sups disliked regulars, pushed them away. From Chloe's experience, they just stayed away from assholes. She had no fur, no claws, no sharp teeth, and they'd been welcoming enough.

It was no wonder that the first time she'd settled down someplace for an extended period, she'd ended up working in a bar owned by a vampire and frequented by supernatural creatures.

Chloe was incredibly grateful for the chain of events that had led her to her place of employment. If not for her boss, Charles, she would be dead by now.

She didn't know why it had taken so long, but someone had finally placed a hit on her, and now thugs were trying to hurt her.

The families of her father's victims weren't satisfied with her apologies, her money, or the fact that George was on death row, waiting for his comeuppance. They wanted her life as payment for the ones George had taken from them.

Chloe didn't know who had raised the bounty; any of the dozens of people her father had wronged could have been responsible. Charles was still looking into it. But she'd been attacked seven times in the last month.

After the first incident, Charles put a close protection officer on duty around her at all times—that meant hiring three guards who could take turns. He couldn't keep those resources focused on one waitress forever.

She'd expected him to fire her, or just tell her to sort out her mess herself. Instead, the vampire who ruled over the supernatural factions of NOLA waved his fairy godmother's wand and made her wildest dreams come true. All right, not literally—although Chloe would have been surprised if Charles didn't own a wand, or a fairy costume. The man loved his masquerades.

Even in her youth, as sure as she'd been of her own intellect, her GPA, her list of extracurricular activities, there was one college she never would have applied to, knowing she had zero chance of being accepted.

The Institute of Supernatural Studies.

She didn't even qualify, because any submission needed to be sponsored by two supernaturals, and she'd known none in her teens.

The Institute was one of only a handful of colleges run by sups, and its alumni ruled the world. Not many regulars were accepted, but those who graduated with one of the Institute's degrees became presidents, Fortune 500 owners, foreign diplomats. Even the occasional king.

Chloe never truly gave up on her aspirations; it wasn't in her nature. She'd always wanted to be successful, driven by a need to prove herself, so she signed up for online undergrad studies after her father's arrest. She had a hard time paying for the tuition and studying while working full time to support herself, but she finally got her BA last year.

She'd toyed with the idea of starting a post-grad course. It wouldn't hurt. If she had an MBA, maybe someday Charles would promote her within his small empire. Never in a thousand years would she have thought that she'd get to work on her degree at the Institute.

"It's a fortress," Charles had told her. "No human can reach you there. I made a few phone calls. Chelle likes you; she said she'd vouch for you too."

To the rest of the world, Chelle was Michelle White, the queen of the witch covens of Louisiana and a frequent customer at Sucker Punch, the bar where Chloe worked.

Chloe liked Chelle, if only because the woman was kind, tipped well, and never acted superior, but they didn't know each other well. The one true interaction between them had been over a year ago, when Miss Prissy Paws, Chloe's seventeen-year-old cat, had been ill. Chloe took her to the vet, and the scans revealed a foot-long list of issues associated with her eyes. They said the kind thing would have been to put her down.

Chloe couldn't even recall a time when she hadn't had Priss. She didn't even think. The pet carrier against her chest, she walked right out of the vet and into Michelle White's distinguished home.

She'd left without her cat. Because the moment Priss had come to, after the healing, she'd jumped on Chelle's lap and claimed a new owner.

Animals took to witches, sometimes. Chelle apologized profusely, but Chloe had just been glad Priss was healthy and happy.

Still. That the queen would go through the trouble of writing her a recommendation blew her mind.

Chloe had refused to let herself believe that her luck could finally have turned, that she could really have a future—a good one that didn't involve her killing her back, legs, and wrists while sleazy assholes called her names and touched her ass. She didn't have a thing against waitresses—they were practically saints for putting up with the amount of crap customers dished out at them—but God, she really, really didn't want to do it until retirement.

Telling herself that she might get into the Institute, and then having to face disappointment when the refusal came, was not something she wanted to go through again.

But the letter that had arrived from England had started with "Congratulations."

If someone had told her seven years ago that she'd be admitted to the Institute someday, she would have snorted and recommended that they lay off dodgy mushrooms.

There were a lot of things she wouldn't have foreseen back then.

Now she was heading to another country, where the name George Miller meant nothing, and Chloe Miller, even less.

This was a chance, a new beginning, and she wasn't messing it up. Even if it killed her.

CHLOE GRINNED AS THE CUSTOMS EMPLOYEE STAMPED the very first inked logo onto her brand-new passport.

"Welcome to London, miss."

He smiled pleasantly as he handed the documents back to her.

"Thank you. Glad to be here. Anything I shouldn't miss while I'm in the city?"

It occurred to her then that the tall, handsome man with sun-kissed skin, Indian features, and a delightful British accent was part of the border force, not a tourist guide, but, as always, her tongue had worked faster than her brain.

The man leaned forward, lowering his voice to a whisper.

"You want to take a hop-on hop-off tour; it'll stop at every landmark so you can get off and visit. And if you're into that sort of thing," he added with a wink, "there's also ghost tours."

She beamed, glad she'd asked. *Ghost tours.*

"Thank you, Henry," she said, glancing at his name tag. "You have a good day."

"Same to you, miss."

He tilted his hat and rearranged his features into a severe expression before calling the next traveler forward.

As she only had a backpack, she headed right out of the terminal and took the train from Heathrow to Paddington, in great spirits and ready to immerse herself in the unfamiliar city.

Chloe had slept most of the six-hour flight, which had left at seven in the evening and arrived at seven the next morning. What a headache. It was now one in the morning back in Louisiana, and if she hadn't crashed, the jet lag would have been a thousand times worse.

She felt a wave of gratitude toward the stranger

who'd written the highly detailed correspondence to her. Along with her acceptance letter, the Institute had added a thick envelope with the most useful welcome pack she'd ever seen. Bubbliness oozed from each of the three pages of longhand advice written on thick, grained paper by someone named Blair Lawson, who perfumed her letters and sealed them with wax and a bit of lavender.

Blair was Chloe's mentor. On the first line of her long message, she informed Chloe that this was her second time mentoring, and that the subject of her first mentee should never, ever be mentioned. And then, she merrily launched into what she called the "Survival Manual 101."

Bullet point seventeen said, "Travel: crash on your way to Europe. As a general rule, I find that if I'm going to the right side of the globe, I need to sleep and bring on the coffee."

Chloe hadn't been sure she'd be able to sleep in the plane, but the comfortable business-class seats were better than her bed back home.

She owed that, and so much more, to her boss. She never would have been able to pay for the cross-Atlantic travel on such short notice, on top of all her expenses. The school was funded by its alumni and didn't accept tuition fees from students, but still, the dorms and meal plans hadn't been cheap. Charles had made it a non-issue on the very day she received her acceptance letter.

"Chelle and I are your sponsors. You need something, you let us know. I'll book your tickets to London. From there, one of Chelle's contacts will pick you up and take you to the Institute."

"Will I have time to see the city?"

Chloe had felt pretty selfish the moment the words had crossed her mouth. She owed Charles and Chelle enough, and this wasn't a vacation—she was being hidden because her family's mess had blown up in her face.

Charles had just shrugged. "For a couple of days, sure. Wear a hat, no pictures on social media, and you're good. I don't think whoever's looking for you will think to check another country quite yet. Chelle will give you an address. When you're ready, head there."

So now, she had two days to enjoy London.

The City of Blood

C hloe didn't think that two months in the city would have been enough. She loved standing in the middle of the bridges, fresh air on her skin, watching the River Thames.

She visited Parliament, Buckingham Palace, and the Tower of London, and wished she also had time for Hampton Court, Windsor, and Kensington. She watched three plays, two ballet performances, and a pantomime —seeing one of those was enough to realize that she didn't need to watch any more. She might have loved it at six years old, though. Chloe ate at an Indian restaurant—the best kind of British food, according to everyone she talked to at the Bayswatter hostel where she crashed at night—and had Sunday lunch at a pub, as well as a fish and chips in the street.

Her first weekend abroad would have been perfect, if January wasn't so very cold. Thirty-two to forty degrees —or, in Europe, zero to four degrees. She was great with numbers, but getting used to thinking in pounds, grams, and Celsius would take a while.

The two days practically flew by, and then she had to return to reality—a reality where she was knocking on a witch coven's door to find someone who'd take her to a college mostly accepting supernatural creatures. It was time to head to the Institute.

Chloe should have been afraid, like any normal person. But if she searched her feelings, she only found anticipation.

As she neared the address Charles had given her, she grew more surprised, and slightly concerned that she might have wandered into the wrong area. The neighborhood definitely didn't look like her idea of a witch's coven.

In New Orleans, the witches didn't even attempt to blend in. Their houses were painted red or black or purple, and mysterious signs hung on their doors. But the quiet residential street off Regent's Park Road in Primrose Hill could hardly have been more inconspicuous, with rows of identical handsome white houses with tiny enclosed gardens at the front barely wider than the sidewalk.

Something felt wrong.

At Number 87, her destination, Chloe found the little gate of the half-meter-tall black fence around the miniscule lawn open. She looked up toward the house. A couple of steps led to a dark green front door that was also ajar.

There wasn't anything wrong with leaving your door open, per se. Chloe had been guilty of that plenty of times back in her small town. But one wouldn't expect that type of behavior in a city. Besides, a bad feeling had been making her stomach churn since the moment she'd turned onto the residential street.

After a moment of hesitation, Chloe pulled her phone from her pocket, finger hovering over Charles's number. Not that he could do anything from all the way back in the States, but if anything happened to her, at least he'd know.

Chloe felt her heart beating in her ears as she crossed the paved path. At the door, she gasped.

There was a body. A person, definitely dead, judging by the amount of blood coagulating on the carpeted floor. Then, her eyes traveled further into the house to see that the body wasn't alone. There were two others just in the hallway: a man pinned to the wall by a long knife, and a woman on her back. Chloe couldn't see any wounds from where she stood, but the absolute stillness was telling.

Never mind Charles. She had to call the police. What number should she dial on this side of the world? She was pretty sure it wasn't 911. Shit, she definitely should know this. Maybe she'd tell Blair to include it in her survival manual...if she actually made it to the Institute. The murderer of those three people might still be here, looking at her right now with a smile on his lips, glad to have another prey. Perhaps the families of her father's victims would be happy to hear the news.

She forced that thought away, concentrating instead on the closest corpse, not a foot away from her toes.

The body in the hallway, right in front of the door, belonged to a broad, bald man with tattoos at the back of his skull. Chloe leaned forward.

"You don't want to touch that door."

She turned toward the low, suave voice, and found a man standing behind her.

He wore a sharp black suit with a pristine white shirt

and gold cufflinks. She was used to attractive people of all sexes—sups had a tendency to look better than your average Joe, probably thanks to some kind of magic. But he wasn't attractive. He was *ridiculous*.

The concept of a man who looked like him should have been entirely absurd. The stranger would have made anyone drool—man or woman, young or old, whether they were into gruff lumberjacks or clean businessmen.

He had a strange complexion, not quite olive, definitely not entirely white either. She would have guessed he tanned well in the sun, unlike her. His eyes were dark and dangerous, but not as dangerous as his mouth. The things she could do to that mouth! And she'd just seen dead bodies. A new development for her, but she was pretty certain that dead bodies did nothing for her libido. She should not have been in a state to appreciate beauty. His hair was long and brushed back neatly, his facial hair carefully trimmed. Wildness and control, merged into one perfect man.

No, not *man*. No man strode quite so confidently. No man made her want to run the other way and leap into his arms all at once. Chloe was a rather simple person at the core: she liked to be friendly and enjoyed the company of people. She'd never met anyone she wished to harm. And yet...something inside her whispered the strangest things. What did his blood look like, feel like, taste like?

What was *wrong* with her?

Then, she realized it had nothing to do with her at all. *He* was doing something, making her feel a certain way.

What was he?

"Not without gloves," the *thing* added. "We don't want your prints at the scene."

The conversation was too real, too casual. Chloe would have liked to pretend that she'd passed out and was just dreaming the whole thing, but his matter-of-fact tone robbed her of that illusion. She wouldn't have imagined a man who looked like him and then made him talk about fingerprints.

He pulled an unexpected object out of his pocket: a phone. His hands would have been better suited to holding a dagger, or at least a gun.

"It's me," he said into the receiver. "Rose's Coven, on the hill. Send a clean-up team and call the humans on your leash. It doesn't look good, but I can't stay to investigate." After a beat, the stranger added, "Keep me updated," and hung up.

Chloe's eyes were locked on him during the whole exchange, because it beat looking at corpses. Now she glanced back toward the house.

Oh God. Until now, she'd held her breath, but now she'd made the mistake of inhaling.

She was going to throw up. That *smell*. What was that smell? Again, she wanted to simultaneously step forward and run away as fast as her feet could carry her.

"It's lucky you weren't here."

The stranger's smooth voice pulled her out of her funk. Chloe suddenly realized that she *could* have been here. *Should* have been. Had she not decided to take a couple of days in London, she really would have.

What was she supposed to do now? She felt incredibly selfish for thinking about herself while towering over three corpses, but there didn't seem to be anyone left alive here, and those witches were supposed to take her to the Institute. She didn't know its location; her letter hadn't provided it. Chloe knew the school was well hidden—one of the reasons why it was the perfect place for her.

She crouched down and hugged her knees, keeping her head low, and breathed in and out, trying to calm herself. Although it was still incredibly freezing outside, cold sweat gathered on her forehead. The last thing she needed right now was a panic attack. She wasn't the one in trouble. She could just call Chelle or Charles. They'd tell her where to go.

"Are you all right?"

No.

"Yes," she said. She had all her limbs, and her blood wasn't marring the marble, so, yes, compared to some, she was just peachy.

"Good. Come on, Chloe."

Her head snapped to the beautiful creature. How did he know her name?

Her heart, already thundering, beat even faster.

"Fuck! You're here to kill me," she gleaned, wondering why her instincts hadn't screamed at her, demanded her to run. "Did you kill these people to get to me?"

The beautiful man laughed low.

"Darling, by now I could have destroyed you a thousand times, in so many different ways, if I'd wanted to."

Oh.

He had a point. She didn't doubt it. There was something so *very* dangerous about him.

"What are you?" she asked him.

The man tilted his head. "You've seen my kind before, if I'm not mistaken."

His kind...

Chloe watched him closely again, focusing on his dark eyes in detail. They had a strange glint, and seemed almost blue in a certain light. And there was his skin, which glowed, too clear and perfect. Airbrushed like he'd stepped out of a magazine. And his...

Teeth. His teeth, poking out under his lip. Elongated canines that hadn't been there a minute ago caught her attention.

He was a vampire.

Chloe understood why she hadn't thought so at first. She hadn't seen many vampires, even though she was employed by one. Most of them kept to themselves, even in NOLA.

The stranger wasn't at all like Charles, who looked like a very strong man, not a...thing. A Greek god. A predator.

She blushed. "You're not a normal vampire."

Chloe felt silly the moment the words left her mouth, but they earned her a thin, fleeting smile. "Observant. You'll do well at the Institute."

The Institute.

"You know where I'm going?"

The vampire looked around and sighed. "Yes, I do. And we can't stand here. Come with me, or make your own way. Your call."

She only had one choice.

A Hidden World

Chloe had done her best to ignore the man—or vampire—whose secretive smile seemed to mock her. He was trying to get under her skin, she could tell, but she was determined to not let him spoil this experience for her.

This week was full of firsts. Her first plane ride, and then her second one from London to Edinburgh. Now, to crown the lot, she was in a train. Not just any train— the Belmond Royal Scotsman, westbound. Better yet, the vampire had paid for it.

Only she should probably stop calling him "the vampire." She knew his name now: Levi, owner of the Institute. As soon as she'd regained her sense, she'd asked him to identify himself, and checked in with Charles.

"Rose's was attacked?" he'd said in shock. "Chloe, where are you? You need to get off the road, right now. I'll send..."

"I'm with someone, actually. He says his name is Levi De Villier."

Charles had immediately exhaled in relief. "All right. You're perfectly safe. Good. Is he around?"

"Riding in the cab next to me, and probably hearing every word."

The vampire flashed his teeth. "Hello, Charles. Long time."

"Sir. I apologize for the trouble."

Holy fuck. Who *was* this guy? Certainly not just the owner of a college. She'd never heard Charles sound quite so deferential. Her boss ruled all of NOLA and answered to no one. That she knew of.

"No matter. Your protégée is in good hands, and we'll get to the bottom of the issue."

"Of course. I'll contact you when I hear any news."

"Likewise, Charles."

Now, to her, her boss said, "Listen, I have to tell Chelle. She won't be happy. She had several friends and family members at Rose's. Dammit!"

Shit. "I'm so sorry, it's my fault."

"Highly doubtful, Chlo," he said. "So far, only regular humans have moved against you, and regular humans couldn't have taken the witches of Rose's. I gotta go."

And on that note, he'd hung up, leaving her certain of what she'd somehow instinctively known despite Levi's dangerous edge: she was going to be okay with him.

And she had been, so far. Levi flew them to Scotland, and she was now enjoying the Highland countryside in style.

The elegant dining room seemed to belong to the '20s, with the cushioned velvet seats, thick patterned curtains, and so many damn spoons.

Chloe was acting like a puppy, and she didn't care.

Her eyes were fixed on the window. If they'd been open, she might even have popped her head out.

And Levi's mocking grin was firmly in place.

"Look," she said, finally unable to ignore him any longer, "I've never traveled outside of the States. It's my first time in a train. Let me enjoy this."

"By all means." He gestured for her to carry on.

"Preferably without your condescending smirk. Being a tourist is no crime."

He lifted the menu to his eyes. "I'll endeavor not to ruin your fun. But for your information, I'm not amused by your novel enthusiasm—if anything, the fact that you've seen nothing beyond your corner of the world at your age is quite depressing. I'm just intrigued by your resilience."

She lifted a brow. "Resilience?"

"Just so. This morning, you were looming over a corpse, and looking quite shaken, if I might say. Now you're effectively distracted. Would you say it's typical of your kind these days? I've not dealt with mortals in some time."

Chloe's good humor had effectively evaporated. "That's called avoidance, not resilience. Yes, it freaked me out. No, there's nothing I can do about it. So...distractions."

"Does it work?" Levi questioned.

He seemed genuinely interested.

Chloe was learning something about him, something that made him feel real—not just some too-perfect, too-cold stranger who might evaporate in a cloud of smoke.

He was curious. He *liked* observing, guessing, and understanding things around him. As a regular, she was an oddity, and therefore interesting to him. She certainly could relate. Chloe had never encountered a puzzle she didn't wish to solve. So she indulged him.

"You mean, until you mentioned this morning? Yes, it worked. This is all new to me and suitably entertaining, so I can put everything behind me. But in the middle of the night, I've no doubt I'll remember him. The bald man. The others, too, but I saw him up close. Not his face. But the smell. The blood..." She shook her head, as if willing the very memory away—ineffectively. "I doubt I'll sleep easily for a while."

Nor should she. People shouldn't be able to see that kind of horror and shrug it off. That was what psychopaths did.

Levi frowned. "I'll have Alex brew you a sleeping draught."

Thoughtfulness.

That was also unexpected of him. Another piece of the puzzle.

Chloe was doing her best to draw a mental picture of the vampire, knowing that he'd fade from her life before she knew it. And she didn't want to forget a thing.

"Now," said Levi, "we'd better order soon. We aren't riding this train for very long, and we don't want to miss dessert."

❧

THE FOOD WAS DELIGHTFUL. HALFWAY THROUGH their main course, Chloe's mouth betrayed her again, babbling before she could question herself.

"Wait, you're eating. Do you guys eat? I've never seen Charles eat."

The vampire didn't roll his eyes, but she could tell he wanted to.

"Yes, Chloe, we do eat. We have bodies quite similar to yours that need sustenance in order to function adequately."

A billion questions popped into her head, but she closed her lips firmly and kept them that way.

Levi grinned. "You can ask. Curiosity is no crime."

"So, what about blood? Is that just a food supplement?"

She wasn't supposed to have asked *this* directly. She knew that. The air changed around them, becoming thicker, stranger.

He smiled broader, flashing his extra white teeth that seemed so very sharp, and she knew the answer before he said anything.

"No. We do need blood. Less frequently as we age, but without it—" He interrupted himself. "Let's just say it's not very pleasant."

She really wanted to know what he meant by that. The need went beyond mere curiosity. Something inside her felt like pushing a little further, and maybe even getting a rise out of him.

Which was insane. And potentially suicidal.

She didn't know much about him yet, but she was pretty certain that those who got a rise out of Levi De Villier ended up exsanguinated and dumped in a narrow grave.

But he'd done nothing to hurt her. If she wasn't mistaken, he actually seemed to be doing his best to avoid frightening her, too. Charles moved a little too fast —she couldn't always catch all of his movements; one moment he was grabbing a pen, and the next he'd written five words. Her eyes couldn't follow the transition.

Levi's limbs were purposefully slow; too fluid and graceful perhaps, but she was fairly certain he did that for her benefit.

So, she pushed.

"Tell me. What happens if you don't get blood?"

His eyes narrowed and zeroed in on hers. They were bright blue now. The warm amber-brown was completely gone.

"Discussing blood with a vampire isn't wise, Chloe."

She shrugged.

"Nor is traveling with one. Yet here we are. You said so yourself, if you wanted to hurt me, you would have done it."

Chloe couldn't tell whether he was amused or exasperated. Both, perhaps.

"Nevertheless, I'll not answer that. You'll study the gory details if you take Paranormal Introduction."

Chloe blinked, her desire to bug him evaporating as she asked, "Can I? Paranormal Introduction was listed in the program the school sent me, but it's an undergrad course that doesn't have much to do with my master's."

"I have no role in the school administration," he replied. "I just own the land. But unless I'm much mistaken, you may study any course taught at the Institute. As long as you don't piss off the teacher."

His language entertained her greatly: a mixture of modern vernacular, with outdated phrases and the occasional slang. His accent was also noteworthy, not quite British, definitely sexy and distinguished.

She had so many questions.

"Sir, we're close to your destination," the conductor said in a low tone.

Levi sighed. "Would you mind asking the chef to send our dessert through, Louis?" He removed a clip of bills from the inner pocket of his coat and handed the man two fifties.

As the conductor rushed to give Levi's order, Chloe said, "Don't get me wrong—as a waitress, I'm one to appreciate a good tipper, but a hundred pounds to rush the desserts? That's, like, a hundred and fifty bucks."

"You haven't had their macaroons," he stated, making her laugh.

The hottie had a sweet tooth.

Who would have guessed?

A pang of sadness hit her. Their destination. They were going to reach the Institute and then part ways. She doubted she'd see him again, not like this. The owner of the land on which the school was built probably didn't hang out with postgrad students. Chloe tried to cheer herself up. She'd meet other people. She just doubted they'd be half as fascinating as Levi De Villier.

Twenty minutes later, after devouring all of her plate and some of his, Chloe understood the generous tip. She was just wiping her mouth, and wondering if she could order seconds, when the train came to a halt.

Looking out the window, she saw more of the delightful countryside in the darkening light. Low hills to her right and woods on her left, for miles and miles. In the distance, a body of water seemed to have caught fire as the sun set overhead.

"Passengers are advised to remain on the train. This is not a scheduled stop. We will be on our way shortly."

That made sense. Chloe found herself wishing they

were stopping for a while. The view was quite magnificent.

"That's us. Do you have your things?"

She blinked. "Here?"

It didn't feel like the sort of place that should be disrupted by...by what, exactly? People?

"Yes, here. Let's go."

The conductor opened the doors for them while the rest of the train remained locked.

"Thank you, Louis."

"Always a pleasure, Mr. De Villier."

And on that note, the man closed the doors and the train was gone, leaving them in the Scottish wilderness. The landscape was so beautiful she almost didn't care that she was freezing her tits off. Almost.

Eyes in the distance, Chloe couldn't stop looking at these hills, this lake. There was something about them.

"Interesting," said Levi.

"What?"

He extended a gloved hand, inviting her to take it.

"Your eyes."

For a wild moment, she thought he was paying her a compliment. Before she had the sense to blush, he added, "Strangers normally need to be shown the way. You seem to have a good sight."

Oh. He was complimenting her...eyesight?

Strangely, that made more sense than his saying she had pretty eyes. Chloe was cute, but next to him, she looked like a charming fluffy gremlin.

"Yeah," she replied with an awkward chuckle, feeling foolish for thinking he might have been flirting. "Twenty-twenty."

He laughed.

"Come on through."

Levi took one step, and she had to take two to follow him. Midway through her second, a strange sensation made her shiver, as if she'd passed through a waterfall. Chloe closed her eyes. When she opened them again, she saw a paved road and a fancy sports car parked right in front of them. Miles away, those hills were still there, but now houses were on them; large, imposing state houses that all seemed to rival Buckingham Palace.

The most imposing edifices were the castle built at the foot of the hill and the house right on top. The former couldn't be called a house at all; it was a fort with numerous towers and surrounded by high walls. The latter was a tall mansion, black as night and shimmering in the distance.

"Welcome to Oldcrest. Come, I'll give you a ride."

The Institute

L evi dropped her off in front of the castle at the foot of the hill before driving to the summit. She wondered if he owned the black house. That would certainly fit his persona.

Chloe expected to feel somehow inadequate when she entered the stylish, antique castle. Meticulously carved out of white stone, with ornate windows and wooden doors with iron bolts, the Institute looked ancient—a new concept to someone from the States. She was starting to get used to it after a couple of days in England, though.

While she'd been suitably impressed by the Tower of London and Big Ben, the Institute distinguished itself by also being surrounded by strange open lands that suited it to a T. London landmarks were beautiful pieces of history preserved in a vibrant, modern city. From what she'd seen of Oldcrest so far, everything here was antediluvian. She wasn't surprised to find that her phone had zero network bars.

Among a sea of olden fixtures, from an actual moat

with a drawbridge around the castle to high city walls and the guard tower, one fortification distinguished itself. It seemed not only old but also unnervingly unnatural. The gates. They weren't the kind of thing one might have found on a normal fortress—if such a thing existed. The gates at the end of the drawbridge were made of a material Chloe just couldn't identify. It couldn't be glass—it seemed too shiny, too precious— and she sure as hell hoped it wasn't diamond, because if so, the two twenty-foot-high doors could buy an entire planet. The water of the moat was reflected on the shiny surface, but Chloe couldn't see herself through it.

She hesitated. Something told her these weren't the kind of gates one simply pushed.

"You walk through them."

She turned to find a woman standing right behind her.

She was a knockout. Ebony hair, long limbs, deep eyes, and ochre skin. Chloe couldn't help herself; she checked her out from her high, block heel boots to the tips of her slick hair. She wore fitted brown leather—not skintight, but still clutching at her every curve.

Then, realizing she was probably being rude, she winced. "Sorry. You're just...I mean. That's a badass outfit."

Breaking into a smile that made her seem a thousand times more beautiful, the woman said, "Chill. Newbies stare. That's normal. We don't bite." Then, she seemed to reconsider. "Most of us don't, anyway. Unless you ask. Do you like being bitten?"

Something vaguely resembling a laugh escaped Chloe's throat. That was probably just normal sup humor, right?

She stepped inside the building and found herself apologizing again. "Sorry. How long is the newbie card valid for?"

The woman laughed. "Case-by-case basis. I'd say, for you, we'll reassess in a year or so. All right, so you can just walk through the gates. They're immaterial. Spells to keep out certain..." She hesitated. "People."

Chloe doubted that "people" was the word she wanted to use. Things, maybe.

"Let me go in first so you know I'm not messing with you."

The woman walked forward, as if there was nothing between the two thirty-inch-thick walls, and disappeared in front of Chloe's bewildered eyes.

Working for a vampire and hanging out with shifters didn't mean that she was used to magic. Sups rarely used magic at all among regulars. She hadn't even seen Chelle and her witches perform any spells other than the stuff they did around the carnival of NOLA to entertain tourists.

Clearing her throat and tightening her backpack straps, Chloe whispered, "Here goes nothing," and walked through the gates. Three steps, and that was it, she was on the other side. As she passed through the barrier, she felt a strange coldness, and the air seemed to resist, trying to push back against her. The sensation didn't last, and then she forgot all about it.

She was in the Institute.

Her eyes widened and stayed peeled for a long time.

To her left was a field of green grass where students dressed like the stunning brunette were attempting to gruesomely murder each other. There was no other way to describe their sparring. They had real weapons—

swords, daggers, bows, axes—and they were swinging them hard against their opponents. Chloe knew she wouldn't survive more than a couple of minutes against any of them, even those who looked quite young.

To her left, two dozen witches were fighting too, but with fireballs, mini hurricanes, and other terrifying pieces of nature in the palms of their hands.

Chloe wondered if she'd be safer back in NOLA, even with the killers after her.

"You look so stressed out, blondie," said the brunette. "Let me tell you something. Whatever you're going to ask, it's probably a valid question. Most of us don't get upset by curiosity. Only ignorance and malice put our teeth on edge."

Teeth. Chloe zeroed in on the woman's. It could just have been the light, her anxiety, or unfounded fear, but they seemed so very white. Bright.

She wouldn't have been able to tell one day ago, but after Levi, she just knew she was in front of another vampire. It wasn't uncommon to come across a shifter or a witch from time to time, but vampires were another story. She knew Charles, and that was it. The rest of the NOLA circle remained in the shadows.

"Are we...are we all supposed to fight like that?"

Hopefully not.

The woman laughed. "You wish. Don't worry, you're not the first regular to come through those gates. The Institute demands the best of us, that's it. No one here will ask you to do anything you're not capable of accomplishing. All right, my students are waiting for me. You know where you're going?"

Her students? She looked twenty, if that.

"Do all vampires look so young?"

The words were out of her mouth before she thought better of it. The brunette smiled kindly, letting Chloe know she'd meant it when she said she wouldn't be offended.

"No, not all of us, although born vampires tend to stop aging in their early twenties. For those who were turned, well, it just depends on how old they were when they became one of us. All right, I have to go. I don't think you'll be in my class, but if you need help, we're all available—any time. Ask for Anika Beaufort."

Chloe felt a little more at ease. "Thank you. Chloe Miller."

There it was, her name. Normally, she saw faces stiffen and eyes narrow when she said it.

But Anika just waved, friendly as ever.

"Have fun, Chloe."

Then she was on her way, moving so fast Chloe's eyes only caught one out of three steps. In no time, she reached the other side of the court and stood in front of a handful of students, who all saluted, hands over their heart.

Chloe's letter had told her to find the entry hall. Careful to stay away from the students with the sharp pointy things, and those with the big, bright, frightening stuff, she made her way to the castle steps.

Straightening her back and attempting not to look as freaked out as she felt, she climbed the five sets of stairs separating her from the main entrance. The hulking oak doors, no less impressive than the gates, twisted on their hinges with a rattling noise. And a good thing, too—she didn't think she had the strength to make those heavy wooden beams pivot.

Still, Chloe's eyes widened as she looked around,

hoping to spot a camera or some sort of sensor. But there were none. Was someone watching her?

She forced herself to breathe out. She was *not* going to freak out because of the magical equivalent of an automated door, dammit. If this spooked her, she was going to have a damn heart attack before the end of the semester.

Finally, she stepped into the Institute.

Wings and Smiles

"Hey, newbie, are you Miller?"

Chloe's apprehension when hearing her name wasn't going to end anytime soon.

"Yeah, that's...I'm Chloe."

"Awesome. Blair," said the woman approaching the entryway, hand extended. "Glad you made it in one piece."

Blair was both exactly what she'd expected and exactly the opposite—a conundrum.

Considering her round handwriting and cheerful, florid prose, Chloe had envisioned a bubbly beauty type with perfect nails, hair, and makeup. A grown-up cheerleader.

She did get a bubbly beauty, with perfect nails— painted dark green—hair—red curls with black tips— but no makeup at all. Wearing combat gear, the woman was more badass than anything else, but her friendliness and enthusiasm were on point.

"Excuse the stench, I've just finished training. I

asked everyone to let me know if they'd seen you, though. I didn't know when you'd make it."

Damn, Blair was taking the mentor thing seriously.

"Thanks?"

"Of course, it would be so much easier if mobile phones were allowed on school grounds, but the board vetoed it. Again. What a bunch of antiquated douches. Of course, most of them are hundreds of years old, so I get why they're stuck in the past. Right, so, it's my duty to show you around, show you your classes, the dorm, and basically be there whenever you have a question. That way, you leave the teachers alone."

Chloe's eyes widened in surprise. "Seriously? You're doing all that on top of your own studies?"

Blair beamed and nodded. "I'm trying to earn brownie points to become a teacher here after I present my thesis. First, they give us mentees, then some minor class to teach, and if we survive, we can hang around. So, I'm not gonna mess up." She said that very forcefully, as if trying to convince herself. Then, to Chloe, she added, "Please don't die on my watch, all right?"

Chloe chose to laugh. That beat the alternative. "I'll do my best. How about the dorm first?"

She was really freezing. Nothing in her backpack was much warmer than the long cardigan she wore now, but presumably, the dorm would have blankets. Her letters had said that bedding was provided.

Blair didn't seem to share her priority.

"In a bit. The dorm is outside of the walls, and we're already here. I'll show you the important stuff first. Do you have a lot of luggage?"

Chloe pointed to her backpack.

"That's it?" Blair blinked her long lashes fast. "That wouldn't fit my boots."

Chloe laughed. "I'm...well, I haven't really kept much stuff these last few years."

Some clothes, two pairs of shoes, her laptop, an e-reader, and that was that. Chloe had stayed in NOLA the longest, but five years of belongings didn't amount to much. Before leaving the city, she'd donated the garments that had aged, and traveled with the rest.

"Fair. All right, no sense in chartering it around; leave it down here. No one steals here. Well, except for Tristan the klepto, but he can't help himself, and he always gives back whatever he takes."

Chloe didn't like the idea of Tristan the klepto getting his hands on her stuff—what if he sniffed panties or something equally gross?—but she decided not to question Blair yet. She slid her backpack off her shoulders and left it against the wall before following Blair. Her mentor was walking at a fast pace, crossing the hall and taking a long corridor.

"First, communication," Blair said. "As you know, phones don't work on the grounds, but they do work in Adairford and in the woods."

"Adairford?" she repeated.

"The miniscule town outside the walls," said Blair. "There are stores, but they sell the basics, and that's it. The dorm is at the end of the village, and there's a bar, a gym, a restaurant...you know, so we don't die of boredom. The closest town is over a hundred miles east, and there's no city anywhere near us, so basically everyone hangs out there unless they get invited to a party on the hill." She was quick to add, "Don't wait up for your invite, though. I've been here since I was a freshman five

45

years ago and I stepped on the hill, like, once. Anyway, I was saying, no phone. For communication, we use these."

She stopped in front of a wide door. Chloe's jaw hit the floor. "You're kidding."

"I wish," Blair retorted with a wince.

"For real?" Chloe couldn't believe her eyes.

"Yeah, I know, welcome to the Middle Ages. Leave the technology at the doors."

"That's *awesome*," Chloe said, stepping inside what appeared to be a giant drafty bird cage where hundreds of ravens were hanging out, entirely free to leave through the dozens of open windows. "Hello, birdies," she cooed.

Some of the birds rushed to her, flying around, and the most curious one actually landed on her arm.

"This is so cool. So, we send each other messages with ravens? How do we do that?"

But talkative as she was, Blair didn't answer at first. Chloe turned to find her still at the door. A short, plump man stood next to her.

"You don't," he stated, somewhat short. "You write your letters and clearly state a destination. *I* send the birds."

Oh. She'd overstepped, apparently.

"Sorry. They're just so cute and friendly."

Blair looked like she was trying her best not to laugh. The short man appeared to have suddenly swallowed bitter lemons.

"Well, you wouldn't know how to spell them to reach the correct destination, so it's my job."

"Of course." Chloe nodded for good measure. "I can't do any spells at all. Regular," she said, pointing to her own chest with her free hand, since the small bird was still perched on her other arm.

That response seemed to appease the prickly dude.

"Very well. If you'd state your name, I shall add you to the register. I'll need a drop of blood or a strand of hair, too."

Stepping out of the bird house, she combed her fingers through her hair a few times without success. Her hair didn't shed much.

"Do you have a needle or something?"

Blair replied, "No need," before lifting her hand and hovering it over Chloe's.

A warm sensation brushed her fingers, and Chloe saw a strange golden light emanating from the woman's palm. Then, feeling a very minor prickle, she watched in wonder as a drop of blood appeared on her middle finger.

Chloe lifted her hand toward the mail guy.

"What should I do with it?"

"Nothing," he replied, with a wave of his hand.

The blood disappeared. "I can't physically store every student's blood trace. It'd be too dangerous. Can you imagine? If someone got their hands on the register, they could track anyone in it with their blood. I just store them in my mind."

Chloe was going to pretend she understood the mechanics of that. It sounded like he had a bunch of files in his brain, and she took the information at face value.

"Doesn't that make your brain dangerous?" she asked.

The man smiled, and not in a nice way.

"Come," said Blair, interrupting their conversation. "I'll show you the cafeteria."

Chloe wasn't sorry to leave the mailroom.

She smiled as she noticed that the bird was still perched on her—he'd moved from her arm to her shoulder. She was surprised the caretaker didn't yell at her for that.

"What was that?" Chloe whispered once they were further down the hall.

"That was Martie. He's a nightmare. Mean and temperamental. But everyone puts up with him because he's the only one who can tame those beasts. Blair pointed to the raven on Chloe's shoulder. "Those birds are not nice, trust me. Martie probably got this one to spy on you."

Chloe glared at Blair before cooing at the bird, "Don't listen to mean Blairy-Bear. She's just jealous 'cause you don't want to play with her."

Blair snorted. "Yeah, right. Are you sure you're a regular, by the way? The raven thing is creepy."

Chloe shrugged her unoccupied shoulder. "Maybe they like regulars."

This wasn't the first time that a sup had questioned whether Chloe was a regular, actually. Chelle had even tested her blood once to be sure. She possessed a little bit of magic, but nothing more than a spark. Chelle had said that most of the regular population did unknowingly have a sup ancestor, often a witch. But with so little magic in her, she wasn't anything special, and couldn't perform any cool spells.

It was entirely possible that the raven had taken to her because of that little bit of witch blood; who knew?

She decided that it wasn't worth mentioning and turned the conversation to Blair.

"So, you're a witch?"

"Indeed. I actually come from Salem, and I'd sell my soul to never return there. Come, food's that way."

The food was well worth the three-thousand-per-year meal plan—the cafeteria was a large hall with many round tables. To their left, windows provided a view of the training court, and to their right, an open kitchen. Some meals and sandwiches were ready for the day, but Blair was quick to point out that the chef would cook anything they required if they didn't mind waiting.

Blair hadn't eaten, and Chloe decided to have dinner even though she'd only just finished lunch on the train. It was so cold out here that the pie, mash, and gravy looked incredibly appealing.

She moaned at each mouthful.

"There's a smaller kitchen at the dorm—self-serve," Blair told her. "If you want your food prepared for you, that's here. They also take special orders—delivery comes every other Tuesday."

"The best three grand ever spent," Chloe stated, astounded.

Once they were done eating, they headed out of the cafeteria and Chloe found her backpack right where she'd left it.

Finally, Blair led her out of the Institute, toward Adairford.

Two Sides

Blair certainly hadn't misrepresented the town. Chloe doubted that there were more than a thousand inhabitants in the hamlet, if that.

The town was also quite charming. On the only street's right-hand side were the businesses—a candy store, a restaurant, a pub, a bar, two clothing stores, a shoemaker, a sporting goods outlet. Chloe made a mental inventory as Blair walked, pointing mostly toward the homes on the left-hand side.

Chloe's eyes fell on a coat: an ugly thing, puffy and bright yellow. She stared at it longingly. She'd need to stretch her savings to purchase a real coat, at the very least, or she'd turn into an icicle by the end of winter.

"That's old Campbell's place," Blair said, pulling her attention away from the window displays. "He owns the pub. His family has been here for longer than anyone who doesn't live on the hill."

The houses were all detached and surrounded by little gardens, but the architecture varied from white rock countryside cottages to dry stone walls and thatched roof croft houses that seemed to be remnants from another era. Campbell owned a two-story brownstone that wouldn't have looked out of place in NOLA.

"The houses are so different. At least I won't get lost."

Blair laughed. "Unlikely. Besides, the dorm is hard to miss."

She wasn't wrong.

At the edge of the village, near the surrounding woods, was one handsome Romanesque white hall that distinguished itself. The building would have been the perfect feature in an eighteenth-century romance novel —a Pemberley, standing out like a sore thumb here. It would have fit quite nicely on the hill, however.

Even in the darkening night, Chloe could tell that the homes perched up there were different from the rest of Adairford, closer to mansions than humble abodes.

"Who lives there?" she asked, eyes on the hill.

Blair sighed.

"The Drakes, the Helsings, the Belfords—you know."

She didn't. "Am I supposed to recognize the names?" Her brain catching up, she rectified, "Wait, did you say Helsing?"

That name she *did* know. From fiction and folklore.

Blair smiled and gestured toward the doors of the elegant hall. "Let's go in, shall we? If I need to give you a history lesson, it might as well be with a hot chocolate in hand."

Her fingertips frozen, Chloe had never heard a better idea.

They crossed a lawn and entered the dorm. Inside, the floor was made of black and white checkered marble.

Black columns stood on the right side, and white on the left.

"Come on through, this way," Blair said, walking straight toward a door on the left. "The other side is for the students who need a little more supervision."

"Minors?" Chloe guessed.

The Institute of Paranormal Studies was a university, but it wasn't unheard of for kids to finish high school early.

Blair shook her head. "No, vampires, shifters, succubus. Those who might eat you if you catch them on a bad night. The rest of us can defend ourselves, but it's pretty hard for a simple witch—or a regular, for that matter—to take on an unstable werewolf, so they're secluded and warded off."

It made sense. Chloe should have felt safer knowing that they weren't in the same section of the dorm, but the fact that she would be living with people even sups considered dangerous hit her right then.

And after giving it another second of thought, she shrugged it off. At least no one was actively trying to kill her. Right now, her mundane world held more perils.

Four weeks ago

THE GREAT THING ABOUT BEING THE ONLY REGULAR human working the midnight shift at Sucker Punch was that no one else hogged the fan in the break room. Shifters and vampires never really seemed to be affected by the change of weather, nor was Margaret, the witch waitress who'd started around the same time as Chloe. A breeze seemed to follow her wherever she went. Lucky bitch. Chloe might have asked her to perform the same charm on her, but it would probably cost her an unborn child or something like that. If the locals knew anything about NOLA's covens, it was that magic always cost more than it was worth.

Chloe had only moved south five years ago, in her effort to run far from the drama attached to her name. When she failed to find a place where no one knew about her, she instead looked for one where no one cared. NOLA fit the bill. The city harbored more sups than anywhere else in the United States. The locals were used to freaks and paranormal attacks, and when they woke up with a strange rash in uncomfortable cracks, they just filed a complaint with the head of the covens rather than waste their time and money at the ER.

It wasn't a home, but it was the closest thing Chloe had to one.

"Hey, blondie. Some tourists turned up en masse," Margaret told her, grimacing. "Bachelorette party. Do you mind cutting your break ten minutes short? You can catch a breather during my break."

"Of course."

She regretfully relinquished the coveted spot near the large commercial fan and headed out of the employees' break room, toward the club.

Like all of the establishments belonging to Charles, the most notorious vampire in New Orleans, Sucker Punch was always packed, and twice as much on a Saturday.

Chloe's eyes widened as she got to the bar. In addition to the two bartenders on shift today, a tall, handsome, and incredibly fast vampire was mixing drinks. Charles himself. It was rare that the boss picked up an apron.

"Is this one going next?" she asked, pointing to the tray of drinks in front of her.

Some bartenders placed the most urgent order on the right side of the bar, and others on the left; it got pretty confusing when righties and lefties were working at the same time.

"Who knows," Margaret said with a shrug. "Charles just shoves them wherever he wants."

She took the tray, glancing at the table number on the receipt. The drinks were headed to one of the alcoves on the second floor. Chloe groaned. Businessmen.

Some people complained about tourists, frat boys, or even werewolves, but Chloe didn't think anyone was quite as rude as successful guys in expensive suits. They believed they owned the world, and everyone in it.

Plastering a smile on her lips because she needed tips, she placed their order on the middle of their table, doing her best to ignore their obnoxious conversation.

"All I'm saying is only one percent of sups go to high school, not even university. They're all brawn and no brain. Have you ever heard of a sup scientist, or astronaut? Vamps are rich as fuck, but only because they live long enough to amass their wealth. We're really the superior species."

What the fuck were they doing at Sucker Punch if they were anti-sup? Charles's clientele was notorious for being mostly paranormals and tourists.

"Now, now," said Obnoxious Two, eyes cutting to her.

"Sups are generally great company." His eyes roamed over her curves, making her want to puke.

Because she worked here, people often assumed she was a sup of some kind. It was no secret that shifters and vampires had a high libido, so that invited shit-tons of unwelcome demands from idiots. Idiots, because if she had been a vampire or shifter, she could have kicked their lecherous asses.

Tips, tips, tips, she reminded herself.

"Enjoy your drinks, gentlemen."

After making her way back to the bar, Chloe ran drinks to the bachelorette party, another alcove, the balcony, and a private party in the back. Eleven waitresses were working the floor tonight, and they managed to clear the orders relatively fast.

Chloe took a second to stretch her sore wrists while the three bartenders worked on the next rounds. She had just started cracking her neck when a pair of large hands circled her waist. She froze before turning around and slapping them away.

They belonged to a large, plastered tourist. He was drunk, and so high he might just fly away. Knowing there was no point in attempting to lecture someone as far gone as that guy, she just pointed away and shouted, "Move your fucking ass before I move it for you."

She said the words with so much authority the guy stumbled in the direction where she'd pointed without stopping to consider that a five-foot-five woman who hadn't stepped inside a gym since high school P.E. would have a hard time moving his two-hundred-pound ass anywhere.

When she returned to the bar, Charles was smiling at her.

Meow, he mouthed, extending his fingers in a catty gesture.

She laughed and mouthed a roar. Ancient vampire or not, the boss was great fun.

"Is this order ready?" she yelled above the music.

"It is, but you're off the clock." He pointed to the clock hanging above the bar. "You're done at one."

She was supposed to be. "Do you need me to stay until Veronica turns up?"

Charles beamed. "You're sweet. But get your ass out of here. You need your beauty sleep."

She wasn't going to make him tell her twice. Chloe practically ran to the changing rooms at the back.

Charles let his waitresses wear whatever they wanted as long as the main color was black. She worked in jeans and tees, because they were cheap, easily replaceable, and cute enough for her to go out afterward without having to get changed. Chloe just grabbed her backpack and rushed out of doors.

She took one deep breath, inhaling the sweet and spicy scent of the city, and tilted her head at the sound of a footstep behind her. Then something hit the back of her head. Hard.

"Ouch! What the fuck, you psy—"

She didn't finish that sentence, because the assailant was dragging her backward with one hand while pulling her hair and wrapping a piece of fabric around her mouth with the other. Oh, shit. Someone was trying to abduct her. Her. Chloe Miller, twenty-five, seven hundred dollars in her checking account and under two thousand in her savings. It didn't make any fucking sense. Unless they wanted to sell her. Shit. Chloe lifted her hands, struggling against the muscular arms of the dude tying her mouth. At least she thought it was a dude. He smelled like one. Thinking fast, she threw her foot back as hard as she could.

"Ow!" Bingo. She'd hit his crotch. "You bitch!"

He loosened his grip, and she yelled as loud as she could, "Help! Somebody he—"

She wasn't even done pronouncing the last syllable when a shadow appeared, flying past her and launching itself at her aggressor.

Chloe didn't have time to see it. She couldn't tell who —or what—it was at all.

The next moment, Charles was walking up to her, flanked by Quincy, one of his security guys, and Victor, another bartender. He pushed the guy with so much strength his body crashed against the wall. Quincy's hand wrapped tight around the guy's throat, and he held him up effortlessly.

She'd never been so grateful for her coworkers' inhuman speed.

"Are you all right?" Charles asked, holding her up by the forearm.

She was a little shaky.

"Yeah, I... He grabbed me. He just grabbed me, right here, from the back, and tried to gag me. There was someone—something—who pushed him away. I don't..."

"Do you know this man?"

She got a good look at the would-be kidnapper. She saw hundreds, if not thousands of people every day in this line of work, but she was certain she'd never seen him. He was the kind of man people remembered. Incredibly tall, muscular, and very handsome.

"No, I..."

"Victor, contact the Wolf's people. Tell them I need a track. Quincy, call everyone. I want all hands on deck. Your phone."

Charles didn't formulate any of his orders like a question. Quincy handed him his mobile phone without protest.

"Call with updates. Come on," he said to her now. "I'll take you home."

They walked in silence, Charles still holding her, half-carrying her. It took a while for her to regain her senses.

"What the hell? What did he want with me?"

"We'll find out."

Charles's lips were thin.

Seven Names

CHAPTER

After a month, they still hadn't found out. They didn't know why that guy, or the others who'd attacked her since, had been after her. That they were hired hands was obvious. But who was pulling the strings? None of her father's victims came from a family powerful or rich enough to have dozens of bounty hunters under their thumbs. It made no sense at all.

And now, she told herself, it didn't matter. She was going to be grateful for the opportunities her misfortune had brought and look to the future. She was at the Institute. Her acceptance wasn't conditional; even if—when —Charles dealt with her attackers, she'd still be an Institute student. It was a blessing.

And she had nothing to lose anyway.

"Common room." Blair gestured to the cozy open space in front of them, stating the obvious. The room contained warm sofas, dark wooden coffee tables, thick carpets over the marble, a large TV screen, and two open fireplaces.

A small group was watching a movie she recognized.

"People!" Blair yelled over the surround sound. "Meet Chloe."

Some waved their hands, others turned and smiled, and two or three, engrossed by the movie or working on their laptop, ignored her entirely.

They walked to the end of the common room, and Blair pointed to a curved staircase carved behind one fireplace. "Up to the bedrooms, down to the study and the gym." There was one door in front of them and a second farther along the wall, closer to the windows. Gesturing to the first, Blair said, "This leads to the back garden and out to the forest. Don't go alone, ever." She led them through the second door and into a large beige and blue kitchen.

"The kitchen is filled with the basics, purchased as part of the meal package, but if you see anything labeled in the fridge or cupboards, it means it belongs to someone. It's not worth getting your paws on it, regardless of how delicious it sounds. Trust me when I say that they'll find out you took it. Locator spells are taught freshman year."

As she spoke, Blair filled a screaming kettle and put it on the hob before opening cupboards and drawers until she'd assembled all the necessities for making a decadent hot chocolate, mini marshmallows and all.

Chloe moaned as she wrapped her frozen fingers around the mug.

Blair said, "So, the hill. It's called Night Hill, and its history goes back two thousand years. Are you taking Paranormal Intro?"

"Definitely," Chloe replied. She'd just started realizing how ignorant she was about this world.

"Good. It should help overall, but you won't hear the deets about this area in that class. It's only covered in Advanced Immortal History. Basically, over two thousand years ago, a higher being went crazy and started murdering everything in its path. That wasn't unusual in that period, because many immortals were killed or banished from this world."

Chloe nodded like she had totally known that. She definitely hadn't. Shit, where was her notepad?

Blair carried on. "But that one's antics were particularly gruesome. We're talking dismembered bodies and blood—a lot of blood."

"Charming."

Chloe grimaced. Then she took a sip of the heavenly concoction and found that she didn't mind hearing about dismemberment and blood after all.

"Well, she wasn't."

"She?" Chloe repeated.

Blair rolled her eyes. "No interruptions. Questions after, if you please."

Her voice had changed, adopting a layer of authority. Chloe remembered that Blair wanted to be a teacher. It might actually suit her.

"Sorry." She pinched her fingers together and moved them in front of her mouth in a shushing motion. "Not a word."

"Why thank you. Anyway, as regulars do, they sent a bunch of soldiers, knights, and heroes to take her out. Which was super stupid, because the bitch was badass. But something happened the day they cornered her. One of the soldiers bit her hard enough to draw blood."

Chloe was dying to fill the dramatic pause with a thousand questions, but she prevented herself.

"The soldier was seriously wounded and should have died."

"But he didn't."

"He did, for a time," Blair corrected. "The next night, he rose again as something different. Now, there are a lot of theories as to what vampires actually are, but we do know they were made by this immortal creature, Ariadne. Legend says she was Dionysus's wife, and it's hard to say where mythology ends and history starts in paranormal studies. What we do know is that she calmed down after making the first vampire. No more massacres are attributed to her. She realized she was capable of creating companions for herself, and she did so, exactly seven times. Drakes, Helsings, Beauforts, De Villiers, Rosedeans, and Stormhales. Those are the families who own the houses on the hill—the heirs of the first vampires, made by a goddess. They're paranormal royalty. Literally. The Drakes are kings of the American vampires. The Beauforts and De Villiers rule most of Europe..."

"Wait," Chloe interrupted her, going back on her word. "You said Ariadne made seven families. That's six names."

Blair's furtive glance went to the open door behind them. The common room was oddly silent.

"Yeah...I don't like to talk about the seventh here. It gives me nightmares."

A flash of annoyance needled Chloe. She felt like she was missing something big—something she *should* know.

That said, Blair had been nothing but charming to her, and the subject obviously made her uncomfortable. She wasn't going to push the boundaries of her first acquaintance in a new place just because curiosity was her fatal flaw.

"Right. So, where's my room?"

Perspective

Whatever she imagined college dorm rooms to be, this wasn't it. The small, second-floor room at the end of the right wing was charming and comfortable but stripped of bedding and decoration. The bare walls were painted purple and had wooden beams, and a four-poster single bed in the corner matched the furnishings.

"That's amazing. Everyone has a room like that?"

"Not quite. Undergrads have to share rooms on the first floor, and we PhD folks have bigger quarters upstairs. Still, the master's students have it good. You have an en-suite," she said, pointing to a door tucked on the opposite side of the bed, "and a small fridge, but if you want to cook something, that's downstairs. We try to avoid setting the place on fire more than a couple of times per year."

Somehow, Chloe doubted Blair was joking.

"The walls can be painted, and you're free to hang whatever you want. There's a service room on the first floor with a bunch of stuff you might need—carpets, lights, that kind of stuff. You should have bedding in the wardrobe."

Chloe looked around. Her place in NOLA had been slightly more spacious, but definitely not nicer.

"That's amazing, thank you."

Blair grinned. "You want amazing? Watch this."

She sat down on the floor in the middle of the room, hands on her lap, eyes closed, and seemed to concentrate. Her pale skin emitted a warm glow. Chloe gasped as her hair moved with a wind she couldn't feel.

"Well? What do you think?"

Chloe was concentrating so hard on the witch that she hadn't noticed anything at all. But when she looked around, her jaw dropped. The walls weren't purple anymore; they were now beige, with blood-red flowers running through them.

"A little too emo for you?" Blair guessed. "I bet you're a blue person."

Chloe did, in fact, like blue. But she shook her head. "No, that's absolutely perfect. Thanks again. You've been amazing."

"And now you want to rest," Blair guessed. "All right, so Intro is at ten tomorrow morning—mandatory for all newbies, be they freshmen or postgrad. Head over to the main court. You need to choose your courses by the end of the month—between now and then, you're welcome in any classroom. As long as you don't piss off the teacher."

Chloe chuckled. "Levi said that too. Do teachers ban students when they don't like them?"

Blair was too busy staring at her in horror, as if she'd sprouted a second head, to bother answering.

"Blair?"

"Did you just say Levi? You spoke to him? As in, *the* Leviathan? Or do you just know a random Levi? Like, Levi Smith or something."

Chloe rolled her eyes. "Levi De Villier. I totally thought it was some sort of a nickname, by the way."

Blair resumed her silent, horrified stare.

Well, as her mentor didn't seem to be leaving yet, Chloe went to the wardrobe and found a duvet on a top shelf, as promised. She pulled it down, grabbed some sheets, and started to make her bed.

"All right. Spill. Details."

"There's nothing to say."

Wasn't there, though?

Chloe wasn't inclined to share the things she'd put behind her. The bounty hunters, the witches, the bodies.

"We traveled together from London, that's all."

"You traveled from London with the fucking Leviathan?"

Chloe shrugged. "So what? And what's with that stupid name?"

"That's his name, and whether or not he was born with it, trust me when I say he's earned it. Whatever you heard about the demon of the abyss? That was Levi, having fun with sea familiars in the seventh century."

"Seventh century," Chloe repeated, slowly.

How old did that even make him? They were in the year forty-three of the Age of Blood, so...

"He's over fifteen hundred years old?"

"No," said Blair.

Chloe sighed in relief. The thought of having met something quite that ancient was terrifying.

"He's over two thousand years old. Did you pay attention when I was talking about the first generation of vampires? Well, he's the firstborn son of Arthur Davell, founder of those we now call De Villier."

Chloe thought about how she'd recognized his otherness. She'd pretty much said that she didn't think he was a run-of-the-mill vampire, and he hadn't denied it. The revelation still blew her mind.

"So, he was turned..."

"He wasn't turned at all. He was born, and then changed," Blair amended. "Most vampires have been turned from human to immortal at some point. But somehow, those who were turned by Ariadne directly are different. They can give birth to children—born vampires. They're extremely rare."

"Born," Chloe repeated, trying to take it all in. "Sometime during the first century of the last era."

"Winter, year ninety-nine. Well, he isn't sure whether it was early in the year one hundred or year ninety-nine. They didn't keep close records in those days. We learn that in Advanced—"

"Immortal History?" Chloe guessed.

She was starting to feel like she should take that class if she wanted to get to know the neighborhood. Which was a crazy notion.

"Right. But my point is, he lives on the hill, comes and goes from Oldcrest as he pleases, and occasionally pops by the Institute's research facility...but he doesn't talk to us. It's like..." Blair attempted to find an equivalent that Chloe would understand but fell short.

"Meeting the president?"

"The president is a lot more accessible than the Leviathan, Chloe."

She was starting to get it.

"So, he's vampire royalty."

"Technically, yes. The vamp queen who rules the northern half of Europe is one of his nieces, Bella De Villier. But even she defers to him. Very few things as old as him are alive in this world."

Chloe grinned. "Do I detect a crush?"

"No." Blair was adamant. "I have a crush on a history and a combat teacher, on a bunch of actors, and the prince of Spain. Levi is practically a god. I'm fucking terrified of him."

Chloe could tell she wasn't kidding.

She paused, wondering about her own sense of self-preservation, because after the first moment in front of Rose's Coven, when she'd rightfully believed he might want to harm her...she hadn't been afraid of him.

Not at all.

"Interesting," was the only reply she could bring herself to make.

A Stranger in the Night

CHAPTER

9

Before departing, Blair told Chloe she'd better avoid casually mentioning Levi around the school. As she definitely didn't want a repeat of her mentor's reaction, Chloe decided to heed the advice. She wasn't one to purposely bring attention upon herself.

Chloe thanked her mentor for the beautiful flowers on her wall, and they wished each other goodnight.

The moment the witch left, Chloe's smile disappeared. A good night wasn't likely, now that she was alone with her thoughts.

First things first. The temperature was warmer inside the dorm, but she was still feeling cold. Chloe finished making her bed, then went to draw a bath in her small en-suite.

Small but delightful, with a cast iron sink and a claw-foot bathtub. She wished she had a bubble bath soak, but she'd only traveled with a small shower gel. She'd have to see if the handful of Adairford shops stocked any. She had a notepad in her backpack she should use to start writing down everything Blair had said, along with a shopping list. First item: decent outerwear.

Fresh towels had been left on a rack. She got undressed, dropping her clothes on top of the toilet, and wrapped the towel around her chest before returning to her bedroom.

She would have sworn she'd left her bedroom light on, but the room was now dark. Frowning, she reached for the light and turned it back on.

Chloe's heart jumped, and an uncontrollable spasm made her shiver from head to toes. A dark figure was standing right in front of her, his back to her.

He was dressed all in black with a leather duster— the sorts of things a bounty hunter would wear. Chloe wished she could scream, but she was frozen in alarm.

Then he turned.

Recognizing him, she yelled at the top of her voice, "You fucking moron! You could have given me a heart attack."

She wasn't sure he hadn't.

Levi just seemed amused, as was apparently his way. He lifted a small object in his hand.

"I promised, I deliver. I'm nothing if not a man of my word."

On closer inspection, the object was a flask containing a clear liquid.

"What the hell?"

Chloe had no clue what it was.

"Sleeping draught," he said. "After this morning's unpleasantness, I promised I'd have my alchemist concoct something so you can sleep."

Right. Now that her heart wasn't beating at a billion miles an hour, she remembered something to that effect.

"Cool. Next time, knock like a normal person."

Only he wasn't a normal person. Everything Blair had just shared came back to her.

Two thousand years old. Frightening. God.

She didn't see it. Oh, he was intimidating enough, and if power were a scent, he'd be wearing it in spades, but he just seemed...

"Yeah," he said with a laugh. "I wonder how that'd go down with your dormmates."

If they were anything like Blair, it probably wouldn't be a good idea.

"Right, of course. I heard the whole 'Leviathan is the Big Bad Wolf' thing."

"Oh no. Plenty of big bad wolves in the woods. I'm a step or two above that."

He seemed downright smug about it.

"And no doubt you enjoy it," she said, rolling her eyes. "Well, thanks for the...draught thing. I was about to take a bath so I don't freeze to death."

"Is it cold?" he wondered. "Very well. Enjoy your ablution. The draught is to be taken when you're quite ready to sleep, and I recommend you set two or three alarm clocks, to be safe."

"I will. Thanks ag—"

She never finished that sentence. One instant, he was right there in front of her. The next, there was shadowy smoke, and then nothing at all.

Well, he certainly knew how to make an entrance. And a departure.

One Step at a Time

The hot water was delightful, breathing life back into her frozen limbs. Chloe remained in the tub long after her skin had begun to wrinkle, until the scalding hot bath was lukewarm. Finally, she forced herself to get out. The bedroom's temperature seemed quite adequate now that she wasn't in danger of frostbite. She sat on her bed and took the translucent flask in her hands, eyeing it mistrustfully.

She'd tried melatonin, valerian, and various sleeping aids in the past. After her father's arrest, her doctor had even prescribed her the stronger stuff. Nothing had worked.

"Oh well."

There was no harm in trying. Already, she was replaying the events of the day, and she could feel it happening. The trembling hands, the flashes through her mind. Her brain was an asshole. It always replayed traumatic events so accurately, as if trying to show her things she should have done, details she'd missed the first time.

Like the smell. The corpse's smell had been heady and sickening, but also strangely...intriguing.

Chloe uncapped the flask and drank it in one go, throwing her head back. It either would work, or it—

※

She groaned, feeling around herself for the offending device screaming in her ear. Opening her eyes to see what she was doing might have helped, but she did her best to keep them closed as long as possible.

Finally, fingers closing around her phone, she peeked at it with one squinted eye.

An unknown number was calling. Chloe sighed. This was a brand-new phone with a sim card from the UK. Surely, spammers hadn't gotten their hands on the number yet.

Reluctantly, she pressed the green icon.

"Miller."

"I'm your alarm clock," said an unknown, irritable, and somehow menacing male voice.

"What?"

"You're welcome."

On that note, the rude stranger hung up. Chloe stared at the phone in disbelief for a good half second. Then, her eyes actually took in the time displayed on the screen, and she jumped to her feet.

Shitty cake! Nine-thirty. Walking from the Institute to the dorms had taken a good half hour with Blair the previous day. She was late on her first official day.

Chloe brushed her teeth with one hand and her hair with the other. She didn't have time to check the mirror above the sink, so the likelihood of having toothpaste in her hair was high. She grabbed the first pants and top from her bag, along with the satchel where she kept her wallet and notepads, and her jacket.

Bursting down the staircases and out of doors, she stopped on the threshold, her mouth falling open. Sometime overnight, the world had frozen into a winter fairy wonderland. Oldcrest had seemed beautiful the previous day, but covered in fresh snow, it was the most enchanting place in the world. All right, she might not have seen much of the world, but the picturesque scene was hard to beat.

She didn't have time to appreciate it. Nine forty-seven. She had thirteen minutes.

"What are you doing?" a guy asked from the threshold.

She hadn't noticed him standing there. She took him in with a glance. He was her age, perhaps slightly older, and wore gray suit pants, a black tank top, and a halter fitted with two guns.

A billion questions came to mind—such as, *aren't guns illegal in England?*—but she didn't have time for them.

"Preparing," she replied, crouching down to stretch her legs.

"What for?" the guy asked, but she was already twenty feet away, so she just waved her hand in the air as a goodbye.

Shit, she was going to regret running without any proper stretching. Not so long ago, the two and a half miles heading up the castle would have been child's play, but Chloe had stopped running track right after high school. Her poor muscles protested against the effort, and her breathing was labored, weak. But she pushed through, forcing her legs to leap as fast as they could through Adairford's main street, onto the drawbridge, and then past the strange translucent gates.

She'd made it. Chloe glanced at her phone. Four minutes to spare.

She grabbed hold of her knees and tried to catch her breath before looking around the courtyard.

Unlike yesterday afternoon, it was mostly empty except for a small gathering. Chloe forced herself to stand upright, like a civilized person, and smiled.

"Hi there. Sorry I overslept. Did I miss anything?"

The group was diverse in every way—age, size, color, and breed, no doubt. Chloe would have sworn she was the only regular here, although she would have a hard time telling whether the redheaded guy playing with a knife was a shifter or a witch. Next to him stood a gorgeous ebony-skinned woman who was wisely wearing long pants and a ski jacket. Definitely not a shifter, as they didn't tend to be affected by the cold. She could be a witch, or something else altogether. There was also a young boy who couldn't have been much older than twelve. He had jet-black hair and pale skin. The last member of the group was a bald woman with tattoos on her scalp; she was as short as the teenager but looked to be in her forties.

"No matter, Miss Miller," the short woman said, her voice distinguished and authoritative. "You're right on time for the introductions, if you'd lead the way."

Chloe grimaced. Right. Introductions. She didn't even know what to say. Who was she, really? For the last few years, she'd defined herself as either someone's daughter or a waitress. Before then, she would have listed her clubs, activities, her GPA. Now, none of that applied.

"Okay...my name is Chloe Miller and I'm from Colorado. I left the state when I was eighteen, and I've traveled through ten different states since, but I've never been outside of the USA until now. For the last few years, my home was NOLA."

"I've been to NOLA," said the brown woman, beaming. "It's pretty awesome. And the witches there are hardcore."

"Good. Very good." The small teacher inclined her head. "I believe Miss Miller was sponsored by the NOLA coven. The Institute isn't only a place where you're expected to learn. You will also network, make connections that can serve you for the rest of your life, long after you leave us. Next time you're in NOLA, Miss Kanye, you may want to give a call to Miss Miller and see if she could get you an introduction to the witches, for example."

The woman looked hopefully at Chloe, who nodded. "Sure. I can ask."

"This," said the teacher, "is the very heart of the Institute. We are a powerful force because we have alumni in every corner of the world. Miss Kanye, you're next."

Miss Kanye's first name was Gwen, and she introduced herself as a witch. "I have a strong link to one element, but I'm pretty useless at controlling it."

The guy with the knife chuckled. "That's one way to put it. I've seen water witches call a bit of rain, but that much snow? I think all of Oldcrest is covered."

It was impossible to tell considering her complexion, but Chloe would have sworn Gwen blushed.

"Yeah, well. Miss Paxton asked me to show her my limits."

"And did you reach your limits, Gwen?" the teacher, who must have been Miss Paxton, asked.

The witch shook her head. "I don't think so? Not sure."

Miss Paxton smiled kindly. "Well, we'll certainly establish that in the next few years. Read, your turn."

"I'm Easton Read, huntsman. I graduated ten years ago, and I'm back here for my master's."

Short and sweet. Everyone seemed suitably impressed. Chloe cleared her throat and lifted a hand. "Sorry. Huntsman?"

All eyes turned to her.

"Ah, yes. Miss Miller is a regular," said Miss Paxton.

The expressions ranged from surprise to indifference, but the young boy seemed downright angry.

"Huntsmen are an authority with a worldwide reach. When a rogue supernatural creature steps out of line and becomes a danger to those around them—human or regular—the huntsmen intervene. I understand the United States attempted to create their own institution."

"The PIA," said Chloe, nodding.

The Paranormal Investigation Agency was well known, particularly since their head office blew up a couple of years back. They pretended everything was fine, but rumor was they'd lost most of their power.

"Yes, that's it. Well, your agency was built specifically to protect regulars. The huntsmen act for the good of all."

Now Chloe was rather impressed with Easton Read, too.

"Speaking of."

Miss Paxton had seemed rather severe until then, but she broke into a sunny smile, hand outstretched as she gestured to something behind Chloe. She turned with the rest of the group to see the guy who'd been in front of the dorm a little while back. He was now wearing a jacket, but Chloe could still see the outline of his two guns.

"Jack, if you please."

The man approached Miss Paxton and bent down to drop a kiss on her left cheek.

"Mimi. Beautiful as always."

"Oh, you devil." She chuckled before returning her attention to them. "Mr. Hunter is a legacy here. His family has trained among us since we began admitting huntsmen among our fold. While he is officially a student like any of you, he was raised in these walls. If your mentor isn't available, I recommend you seek his help."

Jack's cold eyes glinted, showing exactly what would occur to anyone who dared seek his help. The man certainly had a presence.

To her surprise, he walked right up to her. This close, he towered over her, although at five foot five, Chloe wasn't particularly small. The man topped her by two heads; he might even have been taller than Levi.

"You're fast," he stated.

Oh. Chloe shrugged. "I used to run track. I'm not as fast as I was, though."

Spending years working on her feet had made her quite reluctant to exercise in her spare time.

"Mh. What'cha doing tonight, Cheetah?"

She blinked. Was he hitting on her, now, here? In front of the professor and all?

"We're having a race in the Wolvswoods. Winner wins five hundred pounds, loser buys beer. You in?"

Not hitting on her, then. He was very handsome, so there was exactly zero reason why she should feel relieved. But she did anyway.

"I mean... How many beers are we talking about?"

She could use half a grand, but she didn't have enough cash to buy a round for the entire Institute.

Jack shrugged. "Two dozen, give or take."

"Is that an open invite?" Gwen asked.

"No," said Jack, shortly.

Then he turned to her. "Wolvswoods are dangerous. Can you take care of yourself, or are you fast enough to outrun a predator?"

"Yes," the woman replied, meeting his gaze.

Jack shrugged. "Then suit yourself. We kick off at sundown."

On that note, he walked toward the Institute's entrance.

The teen introduced himself—he was a fox shifter of fourteen who'd already graduated from Oxford. Then Miss Paxton invited them to follow her into the grand building.

"The Institute has seven hundred and thirty-four rooms, and at any given time, twenty teachers, ten sub-teachers, a staff of a hundred, and three hundred students—meaning that even if every single one of us occupied a different room, half of the castle would still be empty. You will get lost. Therefore, allow suitable time to get to your lessons. Some teachers do not tolerate tardiness."

Chloe felt the teacher's eyes pause on her for a hot second. She shifted on her legs, then followed the group toward the large grand staircase in front of the entry hall.

"You're this year's newcomers—and returners," she stated, looking at Easton. "Some of you are freshmen undergrads, others are working on their master's or doctorate. Your individual requirements differ, and it is your responsibility to see that you fulfill them. Undergrads, at the end of each semester, your attendance and participation will be reviewed, and you will pass—or fail—tests in the subjects you choose to pursue. Master's and doctorate students are expected to present their work once a year, at the end of the second semester. The presentation will cover at least three advanced courses, although the subjects are entirely up to you."

Gwen lifted her hand politely.

"Yes, Miss Kanye?"

"When you say up to us..."

"It means just that. A panel of judges will rate your work. You can discuss the subject you choose with your mentors and teachers throughout the year."

"But if we pick them, how do they translate into getting our degrees?" Chloe asked. "Would I have a Master of Business Administration if I pick the wrong thing?"

"No, Miss Miller," she replied.

Gwen looked as baffled as Chloe.

"So..."

"So pick the right thing."

Red Doors

CHAPTER

11

They were handed a map of each floor along with the schedule of every class taught at any time of the day or night. The folder was ten pages long. Chloe noticed that the huntsman didn't receive either.

"You're to familiarize yourself with the building this morning. You will not be unwelcome in any room, save for the northern tower at this hour. Your mentors are expecting you to tell them which courses you have chosen to study by the end of the week. That is all."

The woman wasn't one to linger in useless talk.

Chloe opened the folded map on top of the laminated manual and grimaced. At least Miss Paxton had warned them. There were a good hundred rooms on every damn floor, five floors, and three freaking towers.

Towers. As an American, she found the very concept of this palace ludicrous.

"Freaking out yet, regular?" Gwen asked her. "I know I am, and I was born into this shit."

Chloe relaxed a little, glad to know she wasn't the only one out of her depth.

"Hey, you know this place, right?" the fox asked the huntsman. "This map sucks. Can you give us a tour? Maybe show us the fastest way to the cafeteria or something."

Easton was done smiling now.

"Listen, no offense, but I'm not here to play around. I need a degree to get a promotion, so I'm getting one, but I have a job outside of this. Good luck, rookies."

On that note, he walked away as fast as his feet could carry him, leaving them behind.

Chloe stared at her feet awkwardly.

"What a dick," said Gwen. "I say we stick together."

The fox nodded, and they went exploring together, opening each door on the ground floor to find classes on the right and study rooms with computers on the left. The first floor was filled with laboratories: biology on the right wing, chemistry on the left, and something that looked suspiciously like magic in the southern tower.

As they'd been warned not to, they didn't open the door leading to the north tower.

Chloe paused in front of it. The door was painted red, making it stand out in the white stone building. Everything else seemed to be either white or dark wood.

Something in Chloe desperately wanted to open that door, but the red paint also felt like a warning. A "do not enter" sign.

"Hey, regular! Coming?" called Gwen.

She nodded, and after a last glance toward the red door, rejoined the rest of the group.

The second floor was filled with amphitheaters. The

lessons seemed to be focused on science on the right-hand side and arts on the left. Chloe would undoubtedly spend the bulk of her time on this floor, she guessed.

Again, there was a red door shutting the north tower away from the rest of the building. As they explored the Institute, Chloe found herself both expecting and looking forward to seeing that closed red door.

The entire last floor was an open-plan library. Standing at the middle of it, Chloe found herself in awe of the sheer number of books in the place. Millions. Hell, there could be billions. Thousands upon thousands of square feet filled with rows of books, and each high wall, up to the ceiling, was covered with them.

"Holy shit. I'm having a *Beauty and the Beast* moment," Gwen mused. "Belle would have a damn heart attack."

"I just need a torch, a tent, and a duvet," said the boy. "Come find me in a decade."

Chloe wasn't much of an academic reader. She'd been one to do her homework, but when it came to reading for pleasure, she preferred a good romance over a memoir pondering the meaning of life. She guessed that the library would be full of such boring tomes, but as they walked past a few shelves, she discovered a humongous section dedicated to fiction—sci-fi, fantasy, paranormal romance, some graphic novels, manga.

Okay. She was totally up for camping up here with Adam the fox.

She zeroed in on a shelf with a few recently released books she'd been looking forward to reading, and greedily piled them up in her arms. She'd have to check the library's terms, but now was as good a time as any to start a membership.

Chloe was lost in her little world, carrying seven books and eyeing an eighth on the wall, when a breath made her turn her head left.

Her mouth fell open and her eyes widened.

There was another red door here, but this one was open.

Her feet moved of their own volition, and before she knew it, she'd crossed the threshold and walked right inside the north tower.

She bit her lip. Dammit. That was the only thing they'd been told not to do, and here she was, going against the rules on day one. That wasn't like her. She couldn't afford to piss off the administration here—not when she'd been accepted as a fluke.

Step back. Go now.

She ignored the voice of reason and remained where she stood.

Chloe looked down, and her eyes widened.

There was nothing; just an endless gray curved staircase as far as her eyes could see. Which wasn't very far. There was no light except for the one coming from the library behind her.

Lifting her eyes, she found that the stairs kept going up and up.

Chloe tiptoed forward and looked down. There was no handrail, no banister to prevent people from falling all the way down from the fifth floor.

What the hell? That was super dangerous.

She swallowed hard and stepped back cautiously only to find herself hitting a hard surface sooner than expected.

She couldn't be at the wall yet, right? Chloe turned, then gasped, releasing the lip she'd been nervously chewing during her little walk on the wild side.

Behind her stood a shadow.

Another vampire, the third she'd seen in less than twenty-four hours. She could tell now. Besides, he wasn't exactly hiding it, with those fangs pointing under his lips as he smirked down at her.

He was staring at her with eyes that shone in the darkness. Chloe wouldn't have blinked if he'd worn a cape, but the vampire had on blue jeans and a light silver shirt under a black leather jacket: perfectly normal attire that did nothing but emphasize his incongruity, his non-humanity. He wasn't pale, but his skin seemed to shine internally, as if fitted with its own internal light.

He was also devastatingly handsome, with his light hair and tanned limbs.

"What have we here? A curious little fledgling."

She might have answered, if she were capable of speaking at all, but all motor function had been halted until further notice.

Unlike Anika and Levi, this person made her uncomfortable.

The vampire was enjoying her helplessness, she could tell. But his visible amusement finally managed to piss her off enough that she found her tongue again.

"I'm Chloe. I started school here today. Sorry, I didn't know I shouldn't be here."

"Oh, but you knew. And you ignored it. Aren't you a bad girl, Chloe."

The way he said her name was a fucking flick on her clit. Embarrassed and more pissed off, she glared. "Is that how you get off? Trying to frighten humans."

For the briefest instant, he lifted an eyebrow in

surprise, and then he smiled. "Not quite. I could show you how I get off, though."

All right, so she'd walked into that one two feet in.

"Didn't Uncle Dracula tell you that cheesy shit like that basically negates all of your intimidating points?"

The vampire's smile was genuine, and so fucking beautiful it wasn't even fair. "He might have. I've always been a terrible disappointment to Uncle Dracula."

"I can see why."

Sometime over the last couple of minutes, Chloe had started breathing more or less normally. She found that when the vampire extended his hand to her, she could move without a problem. She shook it.

"Alexius," a strangely familiar voice called.

Chloe suddenly inhaled hard, as if pulled out of a spell she hadn't realized she'd been under.

Looking up the staircase, she saw Levi stand a few steps above her, eyes set on the other vampire.

"Alexius, meet Chloe. Chloe, meet Alexius. He will not bother you again."

She half-wanted to say he hadn't bothered her in the first place, but something in Levi's tone, almost threatening, made her stay quiet for once. What Blair had said yesterday was obvious now. Levi was dangerous. Maybe even a little scary around the edges.

"Sorry for trespassing."

Alexius chuckled. "It's perfectly natural. You're welcome at any time."

"She isn't," Levi stated.

The blond rolled his eyes. "All right, you're not. He's the boss."

Chloe smiled at him.

"Well, it's nice to meet you, Alexius."

"Likewise, fledgling."

On that note, he turned on his heels and started walking away, each of his steps impossibly fast. Levi remained where he stood, eyes fixed on her. Chloe wondered if he was going to say something, tell her to stay away from Alexius, or—or what?

It didn't matter. Levi did no such thing. For the second time, he simply dissolved into dark mist.

Which was irritating as hell. After a second, she was alone in the staircase.

"Chloe?"

She turned to find Gwen standing in the library.

Another world away, or so it seemed.

"Are you coming? We're going to set up library cards and then head down to the courtyard. It's almost noon."

Was she coming?

Part of her ached to walk up those endless stairs.

She shook her head, willing herself to regain her lost senses.

"On my way."

Priorities

The large, round study was mostly empty during the day. In a few hours, a dozen vampires would be hunched behind their work stations, engrossed in their research.

He'd deliberately asked the woman to come here at eleven so that they could speak privately.

This wasn't the first time that Levi De Villier had met a prospective bride. The first few had been bothersome. Now, he was used to their buzzing around him wherever he went like a moth to a flame.

He drove away those who were easy to manipulate, but the woman in front of him didn't look like a faint-hearted shrew, to his displeasure.

One glance, and he already knew she'd be a handful. Her eyes were a little like his. Cold. Calculating.

She may have been young by all standards, but she was a true vamp nonetheless.

"Your name is Catherine, I hear."

"Yes. My friends call me Cat."

"You're a Stormhale. That makes you, what, seventeenth in line for the throne ruling over the European covens?"

She nodded.

"Do you have friends, Catherine?"

She didn't miss a beat, he had to give her that.

"People like you and me don't have friends," she replied. "We have pawns. I misspoke when I said 'friends,' but 'my pawns call me Cat' would have made me sound like a James Bond villain."

At least she was honest. He wondered how many truths she'd be willing to reveal.

"Tell me why you're here, Catherine," he said, using her full name. No one had ever accused him of being a pawn in anyone's game without his consent.

She crossed her legs elegantly. "Because my family wants me to marry you. I've been asked to make myself useful to you for the next three years, and to seduce you at the first opportunity."

Very honest, then.

"Why did you comply?"

The stunning blonde tilted her head. "It's my understanding that you might eventually become king in this part of the world. Our intelligence has reported that your niece, the Queen of Germania, has very little support from the other families. Her reelection is approaching, and she may lose. I wouldn't mind being a princess, and I sure would like to be queen someday."

In the Age of Blood, the vampire covens around the world elected the rulers who would reign over humans and paranormals alike. When they retired to the shadows, their kind allowed regular human politics to do as they chose, but they maintained their monarchical systems, to Levi's great sorrow.

It had made sense. Before the Great Reveal, most vampires had been either isolated or part of many little covens often at war with each other, fighting for territory, power, or perhaps just out of boredom. Having one king per continent, and a clear system with laws and structure, had considerably reduced the amount of immortal blood spilled without cause. Overall, Levi would have approved, if he wasn't, as Catherine had pointed out, far too close to the throne.

She was right. Bella would not be reelected. No other De Villier was fit to rule. Except him. He was the logical successor, on paper.

"You did your homework," he stated. "You would have also noted that I've never taken a wife. What makes you think I'd change that now?"

Most immortal weddings were contracts, set to be broken within a predetermined length of time—a hundred years, typically. Levi didn't know many elders who'd remained bachelors through the ages. But he'd never encountered a person—male, female, mortal, immortal, regular, shifter, or anything else—who'd captured his interest. He liked to have sex occasionally, and enjoyed the company of some of his kind. But marriage?

His mind involuntarily flickered back to his encounter with Chloe just a few minutes ago. He was annoyed at himself for thinking of her now, but he couldn't help it.

She smelled of some fruity moisturizer and, underneath that, of forest, earth, and rain. Wild and sweet.

She was a problem he had no time for. A problem he couldn't ignore.

Just like the woman in front of him.

"I didn't think you would," she replied. "But my aunt insists. And I was tired of Rome, in any case."

He nodded. At least she was under no delusions.

"Well, you're welcome to remain in Oldcrest, of course, and you're invited to attend the conclave on Night Hill during your stay, Catherine. If you wish to be of use to me, you may join my outings. My assistant will notify you, and you may address any question to him. You will not disturb me during my studies here at the Institute. If you bother me, you'll be on the next plane to Rome. Understood?"

The woman acquiesced. "Perfectly. I thank you, Your Grace."

Levi sighed as she moved away. All the ridiculous fuss went with his name.

Ignoring her, as he intended to do for the foreseeable future, Levi headed to his computer. He placed his hand on his identification pad, and a small needle pricked his finger, drawing a drop of blood.

The system let him in.

As he was here earlier than usual, he took the opportunity to check on the patients, opening a live video feed.

The main camera showed all seven cells on each level of his dungeons. Inside each cell was a vampire. Some looked very young, others ancient. Some were truly ancients, and others just days old.

All were doomed.

Everyone was asleep on the first and second levels. On the third, three of the seven were aimlessly wandering their cells, their gazes void, their steps awkward.

Levi entered a few commands, and bags of blood dropped from the ceiling.

Immediately, every creature in the level stirred, grunting, searching everywhere like animals, and then attacking the bags. Most of the blood fell on the floor. They licked it, mindlessly ravenous.

Levi's eyes never gave away the slightest expression. He pressed on the recorder in his pocket to make a note. "Containment level three, five weeks after contamination. Subjects unstable. Remedy ineffective."

He shifted to the last level, which held only one vampire. A small boy of nine, or so he seemed. He was called Steven, and he was nineteen—not much older. A child, to his eyes.

Levi pressed on the inter-phone, activating it.

"Steven, are you with me today?"

The boy lifted his head. "It's early. You're normally not talking to me before nighttime."

The room had no window, and the boy had been in there for a long time now.

"How do you know when it's nighttime?"

"I count," the boy replied. "Every day, every night, I count. That's one way to distract myself."

Levi scribbled the word "counting" on his closest notepad.

"How are you feeling today, buddy?"

"Same," the boy said. "Like I want to kill. I want to destroy everything. I want to get out of here. And then I want to hunt you down and tear you to pieces."

Of course he did.

"Why don't you try?"

The boy shrugged. "Because I know that when I lose it, you'll kill me."

Levi paused.

"Do you know why you're here?"

The boy nodded. "I do. That's why I'll keep on fighting as long as I can."

Levi hesitated before releasing the bag of blood.

Steven watched it fall, then slowly, carefully, got up and grabbed it. He tore one side with his teeth and sucked on it neatly, not letting any of the blood drop.

Levi watched him. Seven years had passed since he'd locked him up. Seven fucking years, and Steven was still holding it.

The blood sickness that had turned so many vampires feral was irreversible, forever tainting their blood. Those who succumbed to it were killed on sight by huntsmen. The exceptions were the twenty-two subjects currently in his lab.

Twenty-one of them might make it if Levi managed to figure out the formula that made Steven different.

This was his priority. This. No one else. Nothing else. Not kingdoms, and queens, and brides.

And certainly not Chloe Miller. His...problem.

Oaths

"And Art. I'm definitely taking Art. Have you seen what that dude did with his paintbrush?"

After spending the day exploring the classes, Gwen was ecstatic, and Chloe overwhelmed. There were too many choices for her liking. They headed straight to the mailroom, where the unpleasant Martie grumbled a greeting.

"How do I go about sending a message to Blair?" she asked him.

"You write it. Can you write, newbie?"

He seemed, if possible, more irritable than yesterday, maybe because some raven had quipped at her merrily. A small one—the same one she would have sworn had followed her to her dormitory the previous day—flew around her. She lifted her hand and the raven took the invitation, perching on her index finger.

"Don't the talons hurt you?" Gwen asked. "My grandma keeps birds. They don't like me much, but they love my brother. He has loads of cuts from holding them, though."

Chloe looked at her hand. Indeed, the small talons did seem sharp.

"No, I think this baby is being careful."

"Listen, Miller," Martie grunted. "I've had this job for the last thirty years, and my uncle had it before me. We're servants of the Seven. You can't come here and take over."

She blinked, flabbergasted.

"All right, glad you got that off your chest. But I'm here as a student; I have zero idea what sort of tricks you do to send these to the right people, and, anyway, no offense but your job is my idea of a nightmare. A boring nightmare. I have zero intention of stealing it."

"Swear it," Martie demanded.

Gwen opened her mouth to speak, but Chloe had already said, "I swear I'm not after your job."

The witch sighed. Martie smiled and handed her a blank piece of paper.

"Well, write your stuff, then. I'll take care of it."

Chloe wrote to Blair, asking to meet her when she could free up some time, and Gwen did the same with her mentor.

On their way down to Adairford a few minutes later, the witch told Chloe, "All right, I may be out of bounds here, but I figure someone should tell you. Never swear to a sup. Ever."

Chloe frowned. "Why?" She shrugged. "I'm not after his job."

Gwen sighed. "Because you don't know what the future holds, and this sort of vow can be trouble. Martie is a witch. I doubt he had a binding hex ready, but he could have. Your vow means that now, or in ten, or a hundred years, you cannot ever be after his job. Let's say

Martie's tired of minding birds and decides to apply to a job in a while. Then you see that job posted online and you apply to it too?"

Chloe couldn't see any of that happening, but for the sake of the argument, she asked, "So?"

"So, you'd die, if those are the terms of the hex. Or, maybe you'd just wake up with pustules all over your face. Who knows? My point is, you don't want to find out."

Put like that, her warning was noteworthy.

"Wow."

"Words have power. With your real name, your word, your blood, your soul...our kind can shape your future. You have to guard yourself against harm."

Chloe felt foolish and naive.

"All right. Well, next time I say something stupid, please feel free to interrupt and let me know."

"Promise."

Chloe lifted a brow. "Can we promise, then?"

Gwen broke into a grin. "Sure. To you, anyway."

Because she was the weakest thing in a ten-mile radius.

"Hey, look. Sundown."

Behind the mountains, the sun was sinking deep in the lake. Chloe remembered Jack's offer.

"Do you want to go to that race?" she asked Gwen.

The witch grinned.

"Hell yes. And *you* should. Jack fucking Hunter asked you."

The name meant nothing to Chloe, but evidently Gwen was familiar with it.

"Is he a big deal?"

"In London, definitely. He runs the city, with just a

few dozen huntsmen under him. They're as powerful as mortals get, but their numbers have never been large, and they recruit once a year or so. I say if Jack wants to see you run, you show him what you got."

Chloe paused.

"You mean to become a huntsman-thing?"

That sort of thing had never crossed her mind. She wanted a high-stakes position in a successful company. Maybe own a business by the time she was fifty. Kicking naughty paranormal creatures into behaving wasn't her idea of a career.

"That, and to show the rest of the Institute you're not a useless little newbie they can play with. There are vampires, werewolves, and so many other things here. You don't wanna look like prey? Taking a huntsman's challenge is a good start."

Gwen might have had a point.

The problem was that she could run reasonably fast, and that was the extent of her skill set. If anyone did want to see what she was capable of, she'd make a fool of herself. Staying on the sidelines made more sense. Besides...

"I won't win."

It had been too long since she'd run; this morning had been pretty hard.

"That's okay. Just don't lose."

Chloe pondered her options.

"If you don't show up, I doubt Jack will ask again."

Very true. And if she did show up, she'd spend the evening drinking beer with some students after the race —whether she paid for it or not. It certainly beat going back to her room and replaying every single moment she'd rather bury as soon as she was alone. She couldn't hold out hope for another miracle sleeping potion from Levi.

"All right. Let's go before I change my mind."

Circling the dorm toward the forest, they found Jack with about twenty people, most of them wearing brown leather gear. Belatedly, Chloe realized that she wasn't dressed as well as she could be for running in her jeans and baby pink Converses. The snow had melted away on the roads, meaning there was probably mud in the woods. Pink and mud did not go well together.

"Look who we have here. Just in time," said Jack.

Great. Just in time sounded like too late to back out or change shoes.

"Crew, this is..." He turned to her. "What was that again?"

She didn't think he'd asked her name in the first place. "Chloe." She pointed to her new friend. "And Gwen."

"Right. Chloe, Gwen, this is Tris, Chris, Reiss, Ward, Bat, Bash..."

He lost her halfway through.

After the speedy introduction, he stated, "So, you know the deal. Five hundred to the winner, loser buys the drinks. No rules, but try to stay away from the northeast—the werewolves don't take kindly to strangers intruding on their territory."

Wait, werewolf territory?

"Whoever gets to Lakehill first wins. Ethan is waiting at the finish line to determine a clear winner. On my mark!"

Shit. That was not nearly enough information.

"Get set!"

"Where's Lakehill?" she screamed over Jack's counting.

There were only three hills—Night Hill, then one at its right and another to its left. Jack pointed to the left one.

"Two miles north. Through the woods, or down the path—but the path takes five miles. No rules. Get there first, you win. Got it?"

Definitely not. Her mouth opened and said, "Yes."

"Good. Go."

A Little Detour

CHAPTER
14

Heart beating at a thousand miles an hour, she ran. She had no clue where to go, so she followed the handful of people ahead of her who seemed to know the way.

She'd had a hard time with her morning run, but now it wasn't just about getting to the intro on time; it was about running against people, trying to beat them or at least outsmart them. It didn't matter that she didn't know these lands; cross-country was her thing. She'd always known where to step, how to avoid roots and use her surroundings to her advantage.

In the distance, she saw a girl push one of the guys to the ground. He cursed her out loud, then got to his feet and set off after her. They were both laughing.

Right. No rules. Chloe heard someone catch up with her and decided to veer off the set path. She could still see and hear the other runners, so she knew what direction to take, but at least she wouldn't be tripped over.

Hopefully she wasn't heading toward a ditch.

"What the hell do you think you're doing here?"

Chloe stopped. She had come face to face with a rather tall and exquisite woman with dark blonde hair. She had scars all along her arms and was just wearing shorts with a tank top. Obviously, she was immune to the cold. A werewolf, no doubt.

"Avoiding the others? They're tripping each other and..."

"You know what you should avoid? Getting eaten, that's what. Stay away from the pack. Trust me on this."

Chloe wasn't very intimidated. "I have a lot of were-wolf friends."

"Not here, you don't," said the stranger. She looked behind her, watching the distance. With a sigh, the she-wolf said, "Come on. I'll show you out of here. Hopefully in one piece."

The woman truly seemed rattled by something. Chloe hesitated for a second but decided to follow her.

"These damn arrogant hunter dudes," the wolf grumbled. "They're taunting the pack with their runs around our land, always close to the full moon. Someday, they'll get what's coming to them."

"I meant no disrespect," Chloe said carefully.

"Yeah, right. This way."

They'd arrived at a hamlet, smaller than Adairford, with red brick homes that seemed newer than the buildings in town. The she-wolf put her finger to her lips in a shushing motion and walked quickly along the outer edge, behind the rows of houses.

In the distance, Chloe could hear a voice say, "I smell something."

"That's those guys again," another added. "I tell you, they're trying to prove a point. We should show them."

"Show Jack Hunter?" a woman said doubtfully. "Even if it would be easy to take him, what if his family—"

They left the voices behind, jogging as silently as possible on the pebbled ground. Soon, they arrived on the other side, back to the woods. Chloe could see Lakehill through the trees.

So, the she-wolf hadn't exaggerated. There was bad blood between huntsmen and weres around here.

"I'm sorry. I didn't know I shouldn't have been there..."

"Well, now you do. Stay away from these parts."

She nodded, and the she-wolf walked away.

"Wait," she called. "I'm Chloe."

The shifter watched her, clueless.

"Your name?" she prompted.

"Avani," she said, then returned to her village without giving Chloe a second glance.

Chloe tried not to take it to heart. She was a people person, and most of those she met tended to like her. When someone didn't, she felt like she'd failed in a way. A stupid point of view, really.

Thinking of failure, Chloe resumed her run, heading toward the lighter spots between the trees in the distance, hoping to reach the hill before the last huntsman, at least.

She emerged between two trees at the same time as Jack, who stared at her, baffled.

"No way," he said.

Then his eyes returned to the hill in front of them. A dark-haired man was waiting less than five hundred feet away.

Chloe's brain understood in a split second that she hadn't arrived last—she was first, tied with Jack. And whoever reached the guy would have five hundred shiny pounds right in their pocket.

She didn't think she'd ever felt that much pressure in her entire life. She had to win. Had to.

Chloe's heart beat hard, the cold wind slapped her face and her lungs burned, but she pushed and pushed and pushed harder, her feet hitting the ground like it was her sworn enemy, and finally...

"And that's a tie!" said the dark-haired guy.

Chloe didn't even try to stay on her feet, falling right on her ass and laughing on the ground.

"Holy cheesecake."

Jack, hovering over her, laughed, too.

"Good run, Cheetah. And through the pack territory, too. Ballsy."

"Stupid," she amended. Talking hurt, but she was too ecstatic to notice. "You can say stupid. I didn't know where I was going."

"Whatever. You survived without a bite, that's the main thing."

He extended his hand to help her up. The ground was starting to feel freezing, so she took it gratefully and thanked him.

The huntsman pulled a roll of cash out of his suit jacket. She hadn't noticed, but he'd run in a damn suit.

"We should split the money," she suggested.

Jack shrugged. "Nah, I only run for fun. The winner is whoever arrives first after me."

She inclined a brow, intrigued. What was this race about?

But the rest of the huntsmen were arriving, bearing equally puzzled expressions. Her question would have to wait.

"No way."

"*She* won?"

"Shit. Well done, newb."

"She went through the wolf territory."

Now, puzzlement gave way to horror and awe.

"Holy shit. Did you have to outrun wolves?"

She laughed.

"No, actually. One of them helped me cross the village undetected."

They asked her to tell, and retell, every moment of her interaction with the wolf. Chloe didn't know why, but something told her to keep Avani's name out of it. If there really was an issue between wolves and huntsmen, it wouldn't do to say who had helped her. What if Avani got told off for it?

Gwen arrived second to last, racing fast against a blonde huntsman who lost at the last second. Chloe found herself feeling rather guilty. The moment Jack had said "Go," she'd raced forward, completely forgetting about Gwen and leaving her behind.

The witch didn't seem to mind, though.

The walk back to Adairford was a lot of fun; the huntsmen were into teasing each other, punching each other, and no one excluded her or Gwen.

"Love the hair, by the way," said one of the girls. Natalie? Something like that. "Good luck getting an ombre like that in town, though."

Chloe laughed. Truth was, she'd had her hair cut but not colored. It grew dark at the roots, and then all its color faded, turning to dishwater blonde. Her father's and brother's hair was the same, but they'd both kept it short—and dark.

She didn't mind now, but as a kid, it had sucked.

Children have a way of teasing each other for being different. The prom queen types had many things to say about her bad dye job until she gave up and just started to color it brown.

These days, she didn't care, and no one else seemed to either.

"That won't be a problem," she said, pointing to her head. "Natural color."

"Cool," Natalie told her.

The creature watching at the edge of the Wolvswoods narrowed his eyes.

An Unexpected Bequest

CHAPTER
15

The Snuggy Snot, the one pub in town, was a three-story building with red bricks and wooden beams—positively charming, like so many things in Oldcrest.

"Is it your first time here, Cheetah?" Jack asked as they passed the threshold and entered the warm foyer.

Chloe sighed delightfully, rubbing her poor frozen hands together.

Scotland in January, to a woman used to Louisiana, felt downright arctic.

"Yes. Won't be the last," she predicted.

Jack laughed, gesturing to the bar. "That's old Lewis Campbell, his son Joe, and his daughter Mairi. Lewis left the pack in the Wolvswoods to build this place twenty years ago. Smartest man in town. He's probably a millionaire now. It's the only place we can relax. Most of us come once a day at least."

"Nice!" She followed Jack, eager to ask her questions now that she had him to herself for a minute. "Hey, what was that about? The race. The wolves think you do it to annoy them. And you're sponsoring it yourself with a wad of cash..."

"Curiosity killed the cat," he replied.

Chloe had heard that about a billion times in her life.

She pointed to her derriere. "No tail. Come on, spill. Are you really just trying to get on their nerves?"

Jack sighed.

"Hey, Cheetah!"

Was that nickname really sticking? She hoped not.

She turned to the blonde who'd lost the race. The woman didn't seem to mind. Smiling, she asked, "What's your poison?"

"Anything on tap, please."

"Good girl!" she replied before moving on to the other runners.

Chloe redirected her attention to Jack. "Well?"

"Well," Jack echoed, "I am, believe it or not, not a kid having fun by pulling the wolf's tail, so to speak. I set up races through the entire territory—and yes, mostly close to dangerous sites—because my men need real-life training while we linger here. Sparring in the Institute's courtyard is too easy, too clear-cut. Pissing off one of the most ancient wolf packs in the world? Running close to the cursed caves up in Coscnoc? That gives them real-life experience."

"But that's actually dangerous. They could get hurt."

Or worse.

Jack shrugged. "They certainly could get hurt raiding a bleeder's den in South London, too. And that's what we do, what we'll go back to doing after we leave. I came back here because getting my PhD is a requirement in my position—and many huntsmen followed me. Too many. It wouldn't do to let them go soft."

It made a lot of sense. Except...

"What about me?"

Jack didn't say anything. She narrowed her eyes and crossed her arms on her chest.

"What about me?" she repeated. "I could have been in danger."

Shit, she probably had been. What would have happened if Avani hadn't found her?

Jack shrugged. "I was curious. Besides, the guys push themselves harder when there's new blood in the race."

"You put me in danger because you were *curious,*" she repeated.

"And," Jack added, "fairly certain you could take care of yourself."

She was speechless for all of ten seconds. Then, the blonde thrust a pint of beer in her hand and Chloe did the only useful thing she could do: she drank half of it in three gulps.

Jack wasn't entirely an asshole, but he also wasn't the sort of friend she *should* have. She strongly suspected she didn't want him as an enemy either. Chloe made a mental note to keep a healthy distance in the future, which wouldn't be easy. He was...magnetic. Charismatic. Maybe even fun. But she'd try.

Gwen had opted for a gin and tonic—not the best idea after a run. They were all parched and accumulating empty glasses faster than they should. Really, they all should have ordered a bottle of water before even drinking anything alcoholic, but failing that, beer was a better alternative.

Chloe was halfway through her second pint when Gwen ordered her fourth gin.

She didn't know the woman very well, but after abandoning her in the woods, Chloe decided not to let her face this trial alone.

"Do they have snacks here?" she asked the group.

"Yeah—pork scratching, crisps, olives, that sort of thing. They also cook basic food until nine."

It was just past eight. Chloe went to the bar and ordered ten cheesy fries, digging into her pocket for the newly acquired wad of cash.

The whole lot was twenty-five pounds, and she added a fiver of tip on top. When the food arrived, she definitely was popular. Chloe let everyone help themselves but did her best to shove a plate in front of Gwen as often as possible.

An hour later, they walked back to the edge of Adairford—well, Gwen wobbled—and returned to the dorms.

"Come this way," she said, herding Gwen to the kitchen.

She didn't want to mess with the screaming kettle, so she warmed up water in the microwave and, just like Blair had the previous day, made Gwen a hot chocolate, hoping to get some non-alcohol-infused liquid into her.

"You'll want to put an alarm clock on before crashing," she told her, remembering Levi's advice.

Gwen's eyes were closing where she stood. She smiled happily and nodded.

Right. That alarm clock would never be set.

"Where's your phone?"

She handed it to Chloe. Remembering that Gwen had professed to want to study art, Chloe decided to set the alarm for seven o'clock, giving her plenty of time to sleep off the drunken stupor if she crashed soon.

They drank a pleasant hot chocolate—too thin and not as good as Blair's, but okay—and headed up to the second floor.

"I'll meet you downstairs at eight, all right?"

Once in her room, Chloe closed her eyes and sighed. She half-wished she'd drunk a little more in order to avoid what was coming—the usual replay of her day, her week, her month, her life.

Why was her brain so damn annoying? Anxiety sucked.

When she opened her eyes again, she gasped and marched straight to her bedside table.

There, next to a small lamp, was a package, and on top of it, a familiar transparent flask.

The sleeping draught.

She hadn't expected it at all tonight. She'd been pretty rude to Levi the previous evening, and he'd seemed rather annoyed with her on the staircase.

But he'd sent her one anyway.

Sitting on her mattress, she opened the plain white box underneath the potion. She had zero clue what to expect.

Chloe felt strange—a little confused, very excited, and rather suspicious all at once.

When she was done tearing at the sticky tape, she opened the box to find soft dark blue fabric inside.

She pulled it out and her jaw dropped. It was a coat. Not the sort of coat she could have afforded at any point in her life. A wool and cashmere double-breasted coat with the nicest lining and big gold buttons with a crest. She put it on and moaned in delight. She didn't think she'd ever worn a piece of clothing quite so comfortable, and there was no doubt that she'd remain warm throughout the Scottish winter, even if Gwen made it snow again.

It was so damn perfect.

Too bad she couldn't accept it.

Battle Plan

"All right, here's the list of requirements to get your MBA," Blair stated, slapping three stapled pieces of paper on top of the breakfast table. "The entire prerequisites and curriculum."

Chloe swallowed a mouthful of bacon and sausages before beaming at her mentor.

"Thank you for getting it to me so fast."

Blair shrugged and slid into a seat at their table, plate in hand. "Of course. That's my job."

To her right, Gwen groaned as she massaged her temples. "Can you guys just stop being so loud and cheerful?"

Chloe mouthed, "Hangover" to Blair, who winced on Gwen's behalf.

"Hang on, I have a cure for it somewhere..." She shuffled through her bag before saying triumphantly, "Ah! There you go."

Blair handed a small flask of green liquid to Gwen, who grabbed it eagerly and downed it in one go, moaning in pleasure.

"Thanks!" She gave them a sunny smile, back to her cheerful self. "That's a great brew. My aunt made something like that, but it didn't taste nearly as good."

"Oh, I didn't make this." Blair took the empty bottle back from Gwen and pointed at a G and V engraved in small letters on it. "This is from Greer Vespian herself. She's an *artist*. She's still here, because she wants to study from the best before opening her own store, but anything she spells, hexes, curses, and brews is marvelous. Hell, she makes acne-removal salves smell good."

Admiration poured out of every word.

Gwen looked around eagerly. "Is she here?"

It was eight in the morning, and at least a hundred students were sitting in the cafeteria—a third of the entire student body. Blair shook her head.

"She's on a night schedule because she's shadowing Alexius Helsing."

That name certainly rang a bell. How many men named Alexius could there be here?

"The blond vampire?" Chloe asked.

"The one and only. His kind aren't typically into magic the way witches are, but Alexius is an alchemist. That's a bridge between magic and science, in a way. Greer is learning everything she can from various branches of theurgy."

The two witches began babbling about different magics, so Chloe redirected her attention to the documents in front of her.

Blair had handwritten the three pages in blue ink, and she'd made liberal use of colorful pens to underline and circle certain points.

The contents of the first page were simple enough to understand: every course required to receive an MBA.

Prerequisites: Undergrad degree including completed courses in accounting, economics, management, and statistics.

Chloe had all that.

Post-grad courses required: advanced accounting, human resources, system information, managerial finances, operations management, legal business issues, global strategy, planning and decision-making.

That was...some list.

The witches were still talking, so she continued reading rather than asking questions. Next, Blair had written down the courses taught at the Institute that would help her meet the requirements.

"Leadership, nine weeks, Mr. Crane."

"Advanced Business, twenty-four weeks, Mr. Silver."

"Law: an Introduction, six weeks, Mrs. Wade."

"Business Administration, twelve weeks, one internship, Miss Paxton."

"Advanced Management, nine weeks, one internship, Mr. Everett."

The list went on and on over most of the three pages. At the very end, Blair had added the names and contact details of alumni who'd graduated from the Institute with an MBA.

Chloe had truly struck gold with her mentor.

"Ready to run the other way screaming yet?" Blair asked when Chloe put down the papers.

She smiled, shaking her head. "No way. This is so helpful, Blair. How can I repay you?"

"How about you send me a text next time you're

hanging out at the pub with arm candy? The phones do work in Adairford, you know."

"I know, sorry, I didn't want to bother you."

Blair rolled her eyes. "I live here. Bothering me is doing me a favor."

Chloe loved this place, but she supposed that after years, one could get used to it.

"How many courses can I take at once? I want to see how long the degree is going to take me."

"That depends on various factors. How much you like your sanity, how many extra classes you're taking just for fun, stuff like that. The average MBA takes about three years full time, but...Margaret Lowell, here," she said, pointing to one of the alumni, "finished it in one. She was doing sixty hours of classes per week, fulfilled the requirements in nine months, and took her internship the last three."

Chloe grimaced. She did love studying, but that sounded like a recipe for a one-way trip to the madhouse.

"Right. And if I don't want to extinguish my desire to exist?"

Blair laughed. "I'd say only take one problematic teacher at a time. It's impossible to avoid Silver. You need Advanced Business, and that's his jam—but the guy is a massive a-hole. Paxton is severe, but fair. However, Silver and Paxton at the same time? You'd get gray hair."

She'd met Miss Paxton before—she'd seemed nice enough.

"I have to take Paranormal Introduction this semester so I stop feeling quite so out of my depth," she said. "And maybe Advanced Immortal History, too."

Everything here seemed to revolve around the

vampires, and if the last couple of days had taught her anything, it was that she knew nothing at all about their kind. Hell, she hadn't even known the history of their creation before Blair shared it.

"Ah. Well, Paranormal Introduction is just an hour per week for eight weeks, and there's, like, no homework, so that's not a problem, but AIH...let's just say it would add to your workload. There are a bunch of names and dates you have to memorize." Blair grimaced. "Between the fae, the scions, the dragons, the vamps, the gods, and everything else, that's a whole lot of work for something that won't really help your MBA."

Chloe frowned. Blair was right, of course, but her MBA wasn't the only thing that mattered. She wanted to know the world she'd be part of for three years. If she wanted to belong here, she couldn't forever stay the newbie who asked a billion stupid questions.

"How many hours? How long does it last?"

"Two hours twice a week for two semesters."

She bit her lip.

Blair sighed. "Hey, if you want to do it, I'm not here to stop you, girl. So many people come here with a clear idea of what they want to do and then change their mind one or two years in. Taking a few courses outside of your schedule is smart—it leaves the door open for other things. I was just going to advise you to take a language and at least one irrelevant, fun course per semester. AIH just isn't all that fun."

Again, Blair was the voice of wisdom.

Chloe quietly stated, "I'm good with dates. They just stick in my head without much effort. I mean, it could be fun."

"It won't be," said Blair, grimacing. "But you quite

obviously want to do it. Besides, you can always drop it later."

"Right."

She'd never dropped anything in her life and wasn't going to start now.

One Notable Professor

A ll right, she might drop AIH before even officially taking it up.

This week, they were supposed to sample the casual intro classes before deciding on their courses. Chloe had been fairly certain that AIH would be on her final selection, until attending the class at four that afternoon.

Blair had talked about numerous dates and names, neither of which had frightened Chloe. She hadn't said that the professor was an asshole.

Chloe and Gwen, who'd tagged along, arrived early and sat in the second row. As more students arrived, they frowned in confusion, because all of them were bundled together at the back of the classroom like a flock of sheep.

"Should we..."

Gwen didn't finish the question. A door opened, and a stunning creature with long ears and piercing moss-green eyes walked in. The man wore a long black skirt that floated on the floor like a bride's veil. His torso was bare, and Chloe thanked the gods for it. His body was delicious—golden skin, defined muscles, and a black ring through one of his nipples.

"You. You," he said, pointing to both of them.

His voice was honey and poison, impossible to tune out, so very beautiful that hearing it was almost painful.

They stiffened in their seats.

"I don't know you."

Gwen was stunned into silence. Chloe, who recovered faster, cleared her throat.

"We're new."

"Evidently. What are you?"

She blinked.

"Witch," Gwen whispered. "I'm a witch."

"Mh. You."

His eyes were narrowed and set on Chloe.

"I'm...I'm—"

The words were stuck in her throat. Why couldn't she just tell him she was no one, a random regular accepted here? Then they'd just move on.

"I'm Chloe. Twenty-five. Gemini. I like chocolate and don't see the point in coffee."

Word vomit spewed out of her mouth uncontrollably. She couldn't stop herself. But as hard as she tried, she couldn't tell him what he'd actually asked: what was she?

"Mh. Confused, I see. Or powerful. Well, whether one or the other, know that no power can affect me. None. Not the kiss of a succubus, the whisper of a siren, the bite of a vampire, or the howl of the First Wolf himself, for I am Aos Si."

Oh, right. She blinked. "Cool name."

The class giggled behind her. The teacher's shoulders sagged, and he rolled his eyes.

"Silly little girl."

"Aos Si, as in one of the fae of Sidhe," Gwen whispered, watching him half-fearfully, half in awe.

Awesome. She'd made herself sound foolish again.

"I didn't think your kind lived in this world," the witch added.

Her eyes dropped to her nails, as if she regretted speaking.

"My kind doesn't," said the creature, almost threateningly. "The name is Fin Varra, and as you know nothing of consequence, you will attend this class for a year and a day, fledgling."

He turned away and sat directly in front of them on an imposing gold chair with red velvet cushions that hadn't been there a moment ago.

"We will resume the lesson where we ended it last Monday, after one of you reminds us of the precise point where I stopped."

Behind her, Chloe glanced to see twenty-four hands lift in the air as one. There were twenty-four students in the room.

"Armand."

"Yes, sir. We were talking of the human revolt of 1476, sir. Against the Drakes of Transylvania. We stopped at the matriarch's death, sir."

"Very well. I see you were paying some attention. And so, Prince Dracul's wife was brutally assassinated in his own keep. Works of fiction have broached the subject, but none have been quite fair to his immortal grief. In his sorrow, the prince took his life, leaving two sons and one daughter behind..."

Being a tyrant didn't change the fact that Fin Varra was the very best narrator to ever tell a story—she had to give him that. In no time, they were engrossed, practically seeing the events he recounted in front of their eyes.

Chloe saw Gwen write down a few notes, but she couldn't bring herself to claw her attention away for long enough to get out her notepad. She'd have to copy her notes later.

Two hours flew by at the speed of light, and in no time, they were told that they'd see him again on Monday.

Chloe left as fast as her feet could carry her.

"That was something," Gwen said, stunned.

"Yeah. Something..."

Part of her wanted to bow out of the course; she didn't need it, and this class would likely take up a lot of her attention. But she knew she'd be there on Monday.

She wondered if that was because she liked the class, or if something else was at work.

"You will attend this class for a year and a day."

"Hey, what's a fledgling?" she asked Gwen. The question had edged her mind when the professor had called her that.

"Oh, a kid, I guess? Like a teenager, not quite grown up yet. I think that's also what they call birds when they can't fly yet. It's mostly used about vampires in this world. A fledgling is a young vampire, not quite in control of their power yet."

Oh. So he'd called her a little girl. Nice.

"Can we make a voodoo doll of Fin Varra or something?"

Gwen laughed. "Didn't you hear? 'No power can affect my sexy ass,'" she grumbled in a poor—and hilarious—imitation of the professor's voice.

They laughed until they reached the great entry hall.

"I'm starving. You?"

Chloe almost followed Gwen, who was edging toward the cafeteria, but she caught herself at the last moment. "You go ahead. I have something to do first. I shouldn't be too long."

She headed back to the dorm, took the white box from her bedside table, and walked right back to the Institute, heading straight to the red-doored tower.

She half-expected someone to appear in front of her the moment she crossed the threshold, but the curving staircase was empty. Determined, she walked up each flight of stairs, ignoring the little voice whispering that being here wasn't quite wise.

Irritated

By the time she reached the top of the tower, Chloe was out of breath and her legs were screaming at her.

The door of a large, tower-wide circular study was open, and five vampires were watching it, like they'd been expecting her. Four among them seemed amused. The fifth was glaring at her.

Yeah? Well, get in line, Levi. She was pissed too.

Ignoring everyone else, she walked straight to him and placed the box on the desk in front of him.

"Thanks, but no thanks. I can't take random, outrageously expensive presents from strangers."

It wasn't who she was.

Chloe considered retreating now that she'd said her piece, but that might have seemed cowardly. Instead, she glared at him, waiting for his retort.

"And you were under the impression that coming here to tell me that was necessary?"

She shrugged. "You invaded my place without an invitation. That's called payback."

"Feel free to come by mine any time, Chloe. This is work. I don't care for interruptions."

"Well, tough luck, asshole."

One of the vampires in the room disguised a laugh with a cough.

Levi sighed and closed his leather-bound journal.

"You're the protégée of an acquaintance. You came to Scotland in January with a spring jacket. I don't particularly want to explain to Charles that the student he sponsored died of pneumonia. If the coat was 'outrageously expensive,' blame my assistant. He likes spending my money."

"Guilty," said a man behind her.

She turned to glance at a striking dark-skinned guy who had pulled out a bag of popcorn and was shamelessly watching them.

"You bought it?"

"Yes, girl. I have great taste, right?"

"Yes, it's very...look, that's not the point. I'm a functioning adult, not a charity case. If I need a damn coat, I'll buy a damn coat. I have a credit card for that."

"You tell him!" a woman added encouragingly.

Chloe was feeling more and more foolish at every moment. She'd made a bigger deal of this than it was, hadn't she?

"Well, if I offended you, I apologize. May I go back to work now?"

It was probably past time she left.

"Yeah, sure. Thanks for the sleeping draught, by the way."

"Wait, how does that work?" the assistant asked. "He can give you draughts, but not coats?"

"Because draughts don't cost an arm and a leg," she mumbled.

She didn't think they did, in any case.

The assistant snorted. "Girl, no offense, but the draught, the coat? Same difference. It's peanuts to him anyway. He accumulated billions before billionaires were a thing."

Oh. Well, that certainly explained why he thought it was okay to send her coats that cost four figures.

"Look, in my world, people don't give expensive shit for nothing, and I don't like having that sort of dynamic with anyone."

"And what, pray tell," said Levi, very slowly, enunciating each word, "do you believe I'd want from you, Chloe?"

She avoided his eyes. "It's not okay on principle, all right?"

Every time she opened her mouth, she felt like remaining silent might have been a wiser idea.

"Sweetie," said a tall, beautiful blonde, joining them and opening the box. "Ancients don't really understand human interactions. For thousands of years, it was quite all right for Levi to buy anything he liked for anyone, male or female. Society has changed quite a bit over the last two centuries or so, but it can take the old ones a while to adapt."

Shit, that made a lot of sense.

"All right. Sorry I flew off the handle."

"Good to see you can be reasonable," Levi said. "Take the damn coat and go. I have work to do."

Chloe almost heeled like a good little girl. His tone accepted no argument, but that tone was bugging her nearly as much as his smug, annoying grin.

Instead, she did it again. Let her mouth do its thing without using her brain first.

"Have you ever thought of getting that broomstick removed from your posterior?"

What. Was. Wrong. With. Her.

Blair had clearly told her who—what—Levi was. She really shouldn't have been talking to him like this, as though he were just a random guy in the street.

Maybe she had a death wish.

The others weren't even trying to hide their laughter.

"Seriously, you're just so tense and high-handed. Sounds like you need..."

The next instant, she was hit by a tornado that pushed her against the wall. Chloe questioned why her bones hadn't shattered in the process. Levi was caging her with his arms, teeth bared. His dark eyes were glowing blue.

"You will not question my authority, child. You will not dismiss me. You *will* behave."

Each word echoed around the room, amplified, sounding like a growl.

And for some strange reason, Chloe was...amused. Like this was what she'd wanted all along. To piss him off. And she'd been looking forward to doing it all day.

She had no fucking idea why, but poking the bear was...fun.

"So that's what you look like without the broom-stick," she said.

Maybe she had hit her head.

Levi took a step back and pointed to the door. "Go. Just go."

"I will. As long as you promise me you understand that I will not be bought."

"Chloe, I am so very close to snapping your neck like a twig."

Do it.

What the fuck? She had never, until this day, exhibited any sort of suicidal tendency, so the thought popping out of her clouded, deranged mind shocked her. So much so that she finally did what she was told and headed out the door.

She'd just started down the flight of stairs when her coat flew out of the study, falling right on her head. The next instant, the door was closed.

Damn him. He definitely had a thing for having the last word. She walked down, feeling like she hadn't entirely lost today's argument.

Although it did look like she had a new coat.

Blades and Fangs

CHAPTER
19

Chloe couldn't decide whether she was giddy or horrified at her conduct. She hadn't just acted like an immature, spoiled brat; what shocked her was not feeling like she was in control. She hadn't consciously chosen to say any of the crap that had spewed out of her mouth. Chloe had wished she could blame someone else, something else inside her. Her symptoms sounded too much like schizophrenia. Should she speak to someone about it?

She reached the hall and found it mostly empty; one lesson had ended twenty minutes ago, and the next bell had already rung. She stilled. There was no one around her at all, but it truly felt as if someone was watching her. She glanced outside at the already dark sky; night fell at four-thirty in this part of the world.

She could see the courtyard littered with training witches and sparring huntsmen. Chloe surprised herself, realizing how much she envied them.

She loved practically everything about this place, and

part of her wished she truly belonged here. But she didn't. As soon as she finished her studies, she'd leave it behind. Join a finance firm somewhere. Maybe a bank. A week ago, that would have sounded like a considerable improvement over her situation. Now, she couldn't imagine a more boring fate.

Remembering that Gwen was waiting for her in the cafeteria, she crossed the entry hall and walked in.

Chloe smiled when she saw Gwen chatting away with some of the hunters they'd hung out with the previous day; she surprised herself by remembering their names—Natalie, Tris, Chris, Bat, and Jack, of course.

She picked up a plate of lasagna and a salad before joining them.

"Here's our Cheetah."

"All right, anyone have another nickname submission? I accept applications, please."

"Doll-face?" Natalie proposed.

"Angel cheeks," said Bat, chewing on a mouthful of his burger.

Chloe sighed as she sat down. "You all suck at this. How about you stick to my actual name?"

"No way," said Chris, shaking his head for good measure. "Huntsmen go by nicknames. It's a thing."

There were nods all around the table, except from Gwen, who was too busy laughing at her.

"Good thing I'm not a huntsman, then. Huntswoman? Is that a thing?"

"It should be," Natalie grumbled. "But no. The order is too old to not have a few sexist attributes. But the head of the entire order is a woman, so there's that."

From the corner of her eye, Chloe saw Jack stiffen.

"Really?" Gwen said, eyes wide. "I mean, witch

covens are often matriarchal, because women tend to have stronger magic, but I definitely didn't expect that from huntsmen."

"Throughout our history, we've had three hundred and seventy-four high guard—as we call them. Three hundred and seventy were men. The four exceptions are the most badass human women this world has known. And one of them is his mother." Tris pointed to Jack, who remained entirely stoic and silent.

Ah. There was a story there.

Deciding she'd exceeded her daily quota of nosiness, Chloe stuffed a bite of lasagna in her mouth and chewed slowly to stop herself from asking him an intrusive question.

Gwen didn't.

"How does your ego deal with having a mother like that?"

Jack's glaring game was almost as strong as Levi's. "Just fine, thank you."

Tris snorted. "By 'fine,' he means he lives in another continent so he doesn't have to report to her directly."

Jack chucked his knife right at her. She caught it effortlessly and threw it back before returning to sipping her tea. The entire exchange lasted under a minute.

"Do you guys often throw sharp things at each other?" Chloe asked.

If so, perhaps they shouldn't make a habit of eating with them.

"Just those two. It's fine, they're cousins."

Apparently being related gave them leave to attempt murdering each other without cause. Good to know.

"Don't sweat it, Cheetah. Even if Jack shot wrong,

Tris will always catch her knife and never miss a shot. She's a fledgling."

Chloe lifted a brow. She'd heard that word three times, the first two to describe her.

"A born vampire?" she asked, remembering Gwen's explanation.

Tris beamed. "My dad's from one of the founding seven, so he can, you know, have kids. My parents aren't putting any pressure on me to turn. I figured I'd wait until I look old enough to have beer in any country before freezing my face."

Fascinated, Chloe asked, "Can I bore you with a thousand questions?"

The girl shrugged. "Shoot."

Holy shit, where did she start? "Do you drink blood?"

Tris shook her head after a moment of hesitation. "Well, I don't need to—yet. But over the last few years, I've definitely preferred my steak blue. And tartare is *life*. Dad says if I get to a point where blood smells like candy, I need to turn. Or go insane, one of the two."

Holy shit. Could she write a book about this?

"That's pretty awesome, in a rather gruesome way. So, are you different from us in any other way?"

Tris tilted her head, giving the question a moment of thought. "I don't know. People are very different from one individual to the next. I'm faster than most people, but Jack beats me. Some fledglings have magic, or an affinity with animals, or even the ability to charm people, like actual vampires. My thing is weapons."

Her grin had a slightly alarming edge.

"What weapon?" Gwen asked.

Chloe wasn't surprised when Jack replied, "Every

weapon. She grabs it, she knows how to use it. It's incredibly frustrating."

"You love me, really."

Jack smiled at his cousin. Chloe hadn't been sure she liked the guy until then, but that smile? It explained why she'd been intrigued enough to go on his race, why his confession about putting her in danger hadn't entirely infuriated her.

Suddenly, she realized something: although he didn't compete, the reason he ran with the rest of the huntsmen was to ensure no one got in trouble.

The guy was marshmallow wrapped in steel. All soft inside. He cared about his cousin; he cared about his men and women.

"Hey, are you guys doing another race? I think I could totally use the cardio," said Gwen.

Looking surprised, Jack glanced at Chloe, who shrugged. She'd just verbally sparred with an ancient vampire. What was a little huntsman race?

"Sure. Next weekend. This week is pretty light; the teachers are just reminding us where we were last year while you newbies get a feel for the classes. After next week, trust me, we'll need to unwind."

"Awesome. Can we tag in?"

"Sure thing. It's going to be at the Coscnoc, mid-day."

"Coscnoc?" Chloe repeated.

"The third hill," said Tris. "It's forbidden without an escort because there are some major hexes and traps, but Jack got the all-clear for a paintball race. It's gonna be sick."

Sick sounded about right. "Hexes and traps?" she echoed, feeling like a parrot.

Tris shrugged. "It's just around the caves. We'll mark the area."

That sounded mildly less threatening than a bunch of angry werewolves.

"All right. Let's do it."

Beyond the Veil

CHAPTER
20

J ack had not been kidding when he'd said the first
week on a full schedule was going to be taxing.

In addition to Paranormal Introduction and
Advanced Immortal History, Chloe opted to take
Law Introduction, Advanced Business, Alchemy 101, and
Latin. Blair had advised against taking more than two
major subjects and even suggested that AIH, Alchemy,
and Latin might end up being too much. Chloe hadn't
gotten what she meant, because AIH was only four
hours per week, Alchemy, one, and Latin, two. But she
soon realized that even the kindest, gentlest, and most
encouraging teacher—Miss Penny—gave tons of homework. For every hour spent in class, she had to spend
two or three researching stuff just to keep up. Suddenly,
she understood the sheer size of the library—and why
most students spent all their time there.

It was impossible to research any of the paranormal
courses online, and even the generic subjects were rather
different when taught by a sup.

She'd been warned about Mr. Silver, but the worst

professor was, by far, Alexius, who taught Alchemy 101. The man was a flirt. He flirted with everything—male, female, even with his damn potions—and his students were too busy giggling and batting their eyelashes to really listen to what he said. Then, he gave tests, and when they failed, he sighed dramatically and professed his disappointment.

Chloe watched the whole thing, entirely bewildered. How was everyone falling for it?

But she remembered the first time they'd met, in the staircase behind the red door. She'd fallen for his charms too, then. Why weren't they working on her anymore?

She didn't quite understand it.

To Chloe's relief, she did get along with most of the students in her classes. Outside, she often met the little ravens who rarely failed to greet her, one way or the other. Some screamed from the sky when they were busy with their affairs. Others came to fly around her at their leisure. One, in particular, often made a point to sit on her shoulder and peck at her blonde hair.

She took to carrying some peanuts with her so that she could reward them appropriately.

"You know that's not normal, right?" said Viola, an eagle shifter and one of the students in her Latin class.

Chloe shrugged. "What's normal here, really?"

Normal was overrated.

Chloe did well enough, overall. She started three steps behind most of the students here, but she had one advantage: her memory. It had always been above average, and for what it was worth, her annoying habit of replaying her life as soon as she returned to her own room gave her an edge. She could listen to each lesson twice, and memorize it even better.

She didn't see Levi, and that was a great thing. Remembering the way she'd gone crazy the last time she'd seen him, she deliberately stayed away from the red door. She still cringed when replaying the scene in the middle of the night.

One thing disturbed her. She would have sworn she felt eyes on her, particularly when she walked alone outside of the school. But Chloe knew it probably had to do with the people who were looking for her back in the real world. She was projecting, that was all.

Then she remembered things, little things that made her think she maybe wasn't all that paranoid. Like the "wake-up phone call" on her first day. And sure, it had been useful, but who had it been? At the time, she didn't think the voice had sounded like Levi, and she hadn't met any other man yet. It was all very strange.

All that said, this place was entirely safe from humans. The bounty on her head was irrelevant. Here, she only had to worry about accidentally setting off a hex if she walked too close to the wrong hill. And the angry werewolves, of course.

By Saturday, she was definitely looking forward to a paintball race.

Jack told them to dress in warm, weatherproof gear and meet him at noon. Chloe woke up early and headed out of the dorm with her wallet. She'd been meaning to go shopping all week, but the one true emergency had been buying a coat. As she now had one, she allowed her classes to distract her.

Blair was heading out of Oldcrest for the weekend— she had some family in the Highlands she visited occasionally. Gwen wanted a lie-in, as they'd woken up early every weekday. When she'd mentioned shopping the previous evening while making hot chocolate before bed, Tris offered to tag along. Chloe wasn't one to refuse company.

The woman looked slightly odd without her hunter gear. The huntsmen trained every day, so Chloe had always seen her in leather gear, but today, she was wearing denim shorts with thick wool tights, a wooly hat, and a red leather jacket. She belonged on the cover of a damn magazine. Chloe sighed as she glanced down at her leggings. At least her coat rocked. Never mind the fact that it didn't go with her Converses.

"You look awesome."

"Don't I just?" said Tris, winking. "I got us a ride to civilization."

Chloe was about to ask what she meant when a dark green convertible emerged from the garage on the other side of the main—and only—street. A very fancy vintage car she couldn't name. Jack was driving, a pair of dark glasses perched on his nose.

The cousins really could have been rock stars.

"Our ride, I assume?"

There didn't look to be room for more than one passenger, but the front seat turned out to be a bench with two seat belts. Chloe and Tris were just small enough to fit comfortably.

Jack was listening to blues, somewhat uncharacteristically.

"Everyone's buckled in?"

"Yes, sir!"

They headed out of Oldcrest with the roof down, although it was the middle of January. In Scotland.

The huntsmen didn't seem to mind. After putting up

with the cold for a few minutes, Chloe couldn't take it anymore.

"Guys, it's colder than a witch's tit here!"

"Do you have personal experience with a witch's tit, Cheetah? Because we're gonna need you to spill," Tris said, pressing a button.

"Har, har."

The roof slowly uncurled from the back of the car, and Jack turned on the heat.

"I'd play with Blair's tits," Tris said, shrugging. "And Gwen's. And—"

"Just about everyone in the dorm. We're aware," said Jack with a grimace.

He apparently wasn't into discussing his cousin's sex life.

"Like you don't get any."

"Not in Oldcrest, I don't."

Chloe was fascinated with the conversation. She wasn't blind—or deaf, for that matter. She knew most people in the dorm had no issue bed-hopping, and if she was honest, she would have thought that Jack was one of them.

From the very start, she'd decided to avoid complicating her stay with casual sex, or a relationship. She was here to make friends and get her degree. Banging someone she basically lived with sounded like a recipe for disaster.

She'd been surprised to realize that her point of view wasn't shared by many in the dorms.

"Wait, so the rumors of you and that hot vamp..."

Jack snorted at his cousin. "No offense, but you know what I think about most vampires."

Tris shrugged. "Well, you like me well enough. And

Chris told me you danced with her on Night Hill last Sunday."

"That was work."

He said nothing else, and Tris found no reason to question him further, so Chloe had to be nosy again. "You work on Night Hill?" she asked.

Jack glanced away from the road for half a second, watching her before setting his eyes forward again.

"We're about to cross the border. Hang on tight."

She had an instant to tense before feeling that strange wave of water again, and then they were out of Oldcrest. Looking back, Chloe saw absolutely nothing. Her stomach churned. She didn't like it at all.

Suddenly, she remembered why. She had people looking for her here in the real world. What would Charles think if he knew she was popping out of safety just to shop?

It felt like a terrible idea, and she considered asking Jack to turn around.

"The huntsmen work without needing to report to an authority outside of our order," he told her. "We have an understanding with most governments. Basically, if they want us to protect them, they let us do our thing. The exceptions are vamps. The suckers make us *ask*." His tone couldn't have been more disgusted. "I spotted something funny, so I had to head over to De Villier's place and ask if I could organize a patrol around Oldcrest. The territory technically belongs to him."

Suitably distracted, Chloe let go of the worry. She'd be okay. She was with two badass huntsmen, and the bounty hunters probably still thought she was in NOLA.

"How does that end with you dancing with a hot vamp?" Chloe asked, with validity, she thought.

Jack sighed. "Because vampires have a complicated dynamic. We don't make an appointment. We're guests, and we request an audience with the master of the house. In the meantime, we're expected to pleasantly drink, and dance, and eat canapes until his mighty pain in the arse decides he can be arsed to see us."

That sounded like Levi.

"I'd like to see you dance."

He was too collected and in control, always in a suit, even now, even when he ran. She just couldn't picture it.

"Trust me, you wouldn't. He steps on toes a lot."

"That would be because you're entirely incapable of letting anyone lead, Patricia."

Until now, Chloe hadn't realized that Tris was a nickname.

"Hang on. She gets Tris, I get Cheetah?"

Jack shrugged unapologetically. "She earned Tris. She was Blades for years. Then, she took down her own major demon and got to pick her name."

"So Chris, Reiss, Bash, and all the others did something noteworthy before getting the name they wanted?"

"Not Bash. I picked Bash. He hasn't been in the field yet. Bat, too."

"He goes alphabetically. You're lucky he was done with the B's," said Tris.

She ruminated on her fate to remain "Cheetah" until the end of time. Or at least the end of her time in the Institute.

"Hey, why did Gwen escape the nickname thing?"

Jack snorted as he turned toward the entrance of a car park. They'd arrived in a nice city that seemed gigantic after ten days in Oldcrest.

"Do you need to ask?"

She did. Chloe glared at Jack, ready to be offended on behalf of her friend.

"What's wrong with Gwen?"

"Nothing. I'm just not stupid enough to mess with witches. The last fool who pissed one off woke up with a rash all over his ass. Pass."

Numbers

21

"All right, meet in two hours?" Jack asked.

Chloe shouldn't have been surprised that he'd try to escape; not many men were up for a girly shopping trip.

"Three?" Tris asked hopefully.

He shook his head. "The drive back to Oldcrest from Inverness is a good two hours, and we set up the meeting at twelve. Two hours is pushing it."

"Got it. Come on, Chloe. Shoes first."

Tris seemed to know the city very well; as they walked along the River Ness, she told her about the castle that had been built back in the medieval days and then redesigned during the reign of Mary, Queen of Scots.

"I don't know the history of these parts as well as many," Tris admitted. "Jack and I are from New York."

Chloe had guessed, given their accent. They'd both adopted an almost British twang, but she'd detected an American drawl underneath it all.

"What made you leave?" Chloe asked as they reached a shoe store.

"A big-ass shadow," she replied, confusing Chloe.

Given all the magic and mystery surrounding the world she'd dived into, she asked, "What, an actual shadow?"

Tris shook her head. "My sister. Perfect. Turned at twenty-one, so she looks younger than me although she's ten years older. Very strong. Extremely good at magic. Everything I do, she does, only better. Jack was pretty much fostered at the Institute because his parents were always working, but he left New York a good ten years ago, when I was sixteen. He was eighteen and had just been assigned to London. I busted my ass to get the grades and asked to get into the Institute. My sister studied at the Academy in New York, so that was the first time I did something different. I like it here. I'll stay in London under Jack's rule after I get my master's."

Chloe got it.

The mixture of normalcy, magic, and supernatural somehow made Tris more real. Who cared that she'd eventually turn into a vampire? She was just another woman trying to escape the umbrella cast by another family member. At least Tris's shadow wasn't a murderer.

"I get why you'd want to—"

Stay. She was going to say stay. But her eyes fell on the price tag of the leather boots that she'd been eyeing and she wasn't able to get another word out.

Holy shitcakes, she needed to get out of this store, pronto.

"Not cheap, right?" said Tris, wincing. "But these shoes feel as comfy as any trainers inside, and the leather is the best quality—only gets cooler with time. Check these out."

Tris showed off her own leather boots, which seemed right out of the store. They were dark gray, almost black, but they'd been cleverly distressed, and the part where the leather had been scratched revealed a red underlayer.

"They're seven years old. Trust me when I say I've used them."

"But, four figures," Chloe whispered, eyes still bulging.

Now that she wasn't working, she was only relying on her savings and credit card. Chloe had calculated that she had enough for four years if she was careful. Buying these shoes wasn't careful.

Chloe had toyed with the idea of asking the Campbells if they needed a waitress at the Snuggy Snot. If she caved and bought those drool-worthy boots, she'd need to beg for the job.

"I'll get them if you want," said Tris indifferently. Chloe was already shaking her head, but the woman added, "You can work it off."

Oh. Well, that changed things.

"How?"

Tris thought it out. "You said you had a bachelor's in accounting? We're looking for someone to run our paychecks and stuff. Jack did it last week, but it's taking up too much time. If you're up for it, the huntsmen pay pretty well. You can pay me back in installments of whatever."

Chloe blinked. "You mean I could get a job with you guys?"

A job that didn't involve bussing tables, either.

"Jack would kiss you if you'd take it. Seriously. Not

many people go to the Institute for business, and you already have an accounting degree. He wouldn't trust anyone outside of Oldcrest for this. We had someone in London—a witch-slash-business manager—but the coven was—never mind."

Killed. She was talking about Rose's Coven, which had been wiped out the previous week.

"I'm definitely interested, if you think Jack would—"

Lifting one finger, Tris said, "Hold that thought," and called her cousin. "Hey, Jack. I was talking to Chloe about doing our payroll. Yeah. Yeah. Sure. Totally." She hung up. "You got the job. Part time, twenty-five per hour, and you'll need to sign an NDA. There are about a hundred paychecks to process per week, plus the overall profit and loss account."

Chloe squealed. "Do you have a size eight?"

After she happily charged the boots on her credit card, they went to get her weather-appropriate clothing. Chloe had always been a jeans and T-shirt kind of woman, but the weather made tights, long underwear, and knitwear more appropriate. Finally, Tris ended the trip at a sportswear store, where Chloe grabbed a few exercise bras, yoga pants, and a running jacket. If she was going to race with the huntsmen on a regular basis, it sounded like a good idea.

They ran back to the car park to make it within the two-hour window. Jack arrived right after them with a bunch of white boxes they stacked on their knees and in the boot.

"Is that what I think it is?" Tris asked eagerly.

"Hands off."

Jack was stern.

"Just the one."

"Hands *off*."

"What is it?" Chloe asked.

"Cakes, pies, and doughnuts from the best bakery in town. Jack does that from time to time. Being liked makes our job a lot easier. Say in twenty years he needs info from a random clan, but hey, one of the witches remembers he gave her free cake..."

"There are exactly three hundred and seventy-one pieces, which means one for every person I intend to give it to. *Hands off*, cousin."

"But I could have mine *now*," Tris argued.

Chloe's stomach gargled at the scent of doughy, buttery, and sugary goodness.

"I know you. Take one now, you'll be on your tenth by the time we get to Oldcrest. No."

Tris only ate four. Chloe had five, though.

The Path

U nlike last time, this week's run had a lot more participants; Chloe noticed some younger students right out of high school.

It was apparent that huntsmen took paintballing seriously. Chloe got it, given the fact that another pile of cash was involved.

"The rules are simple: you have to get to the summit. The likelihood of anyone making it without getting hit at least once is close to nil, so the rule is, you have to get hit less than three times. The reward is five hundred. If anyone makes it without a single paintball, I'll throw another five hundred on top."

Chloe could practically feel the excitement buzzing when Jack said that.

Damn. If she won this time, that would almost pay for the shiny new boots she wasn't wearing now. She'd opted for her trainers instead, because it had rained overnight and she wasn't getting mud on her pretty boots the first day.

"Last time we raced, I may have been a tad careless

when I didn't share the whole picture. There are zones marked off on this hill with black tape. You enter those zones at your own risk—it's not against the rules, but the likelihood of you getting out of there alive is pretty grim. Got it? Good. On your mark."

One thousand pounds. One thousand pounds. One thousand...damn right she was a cheetah today.

Chloe leaped into action the moment Jack said, "Go," pushing herself harder than before. Now that she had proper gear that was easy to run in and shoes that weren't pinching her toes, her body wasn't protesting against the effort. The previous week, she'd purposely stayed behind those in the lead since she didn't know the way. "The summit" wasn't a hard direction. She could see it overhead, and although the hill was thick with trees and treacherous paths, the various paths leading up were clear enough.

Hearing a gunshot behind her, Chloe leaped to her right, then ducked and rolled on the cold, slightly damp, mossy ground. She shot blindly in the direction of the sound before resuming her run. The interruption had changed her course, but another path on the right led upward. She took it.

Running faster and faster, Chloe was almost halfway up the hill when she realized that most of the sounds seemed pretty far away. She took the time to look behind her. No one. They seemed to have all taken the left path, which either meant they were sheep or her way didn't lead to the summit. Hopefully the former.

Looking up, she saw the path continue. She was a mile or so down from an intersection, but she could clearly see the left pathway leading to the top. She could carry on and then turn left.

The path got steeper and steeper; no doubt that was why the others had avoided it. But Chloe kept going. Steeper meant that she'd arrive faster as long as she didn't slow down.

She reached the intersection where she should have turned left. One look down the mountain showed that she had at least five minutes on the next closest runner.

Instead of taking the left road, she found herself looking right.

Black tape barred the path, and beyond the tape was only sinuous trees, and then, darkness.

Chloe felt herself edging toward the tape. Where did this path lead? She wished she could tell.

Biting her lip, she took another step...

"Don't."

Chloe turned. A stranger stood in front of her. He was dark-haired and bronze-skinned, with crow-black eyes and a threatening edge. She'd never seen him in her life; he wasn't the sort of man someone could forget. And yet, he didn't feel like a stranger at all. She knew his presence.

"So you're my stalker."

She was strangely calm about it. Why was she calm? Probably because she had felt him follow her from the first day, and he hadn't harmed her yet. Besides, if he did want to harm her, she couldn't do much about it. He was a vampire, that much was crystal clear.

He grinned. "I prefer babysitter."

"You've been sent to protect me?"

Chloe frowned. Wasn't she here, in this territory, because she didn't need a bodyguard twenty-four seven?

The vampire snorted. "More or less. I have...specific orders. I can't let you get drowned, decapitated, or burned to death. If you go down that path, I can't follow you and do my job. And you'll never come back."

Ominous.

"Drowned, beheaded, or burned," she repeated. "What if someone strangles me, then?"

The vampire shrugged. "Not my problem."

Chloe's jaw fell open. What the hell?

"Seriously?"

"Oh, yeah."

She shook her head in disbelief. "Well, it's a good thing no one here seems to be trying to murder me..."

"If you go down this way, someone will," the vampire said, tilting his chin toward the path she was still eyeing.

Chloe sighed. She felt...drawn to it. Drawn to that dark place he seemed so afraid of.

"What's down there?"

"Nothing you should concern yourself with. And, by the way, you've lost the lead. Better get going if you want to win, fledgling."

Oh shit.

Chloe started to run before turning back to ask her bodyguard's name. But he'd disappeared.

She groaned. Damn vampires and their dramatic exits.

TRIS WON THE FIVE HUNDRED POUNDS, ALTHOUGH Gwen didn't do half bad, arriving fourth this time. Apart from Chloe, she was the only racer to finish without any paint on her clothes. She'd been smart enough to cast a protection spell, so the paint bounced right off her.

Someone managed to get Jack behind the shoulder

blades, and although no one was admitting to the shot, Chloe would have bet her money on Tris, who looked far too smug.

They ended up at the pub again, and this time, Gwen stuck to beer.

Chloe thought about her promise to tell Blair the next time they were having a drink with the huntsmen, so, with a fresh beer in hand, she excused herself to use her phone outside of the crowded establishment. She wasn't sure whether Blair had left to see her family for the whole weekend, but she tried to call just in case.

The call went to her voicemail after the tenth ring.

Chloe hesitated as she turned back toward the pub, her eyes darting to the edge of the forest. After debating for a moment, she crossed the road and zigzagged between detached houses to reach the Wolvswoods.

"I have a beer," she announced.

She felt rather foolish upon hearing nothing but silence at first, but after a moment, the vampire stepped into view, his booted feet muffled on the forest floor.

"So I see."

She lifted her hand to give it to him.

"Not my drink of choice."

Oh well, it was worth a try.

"You're on a blood-only diet?"

He flashed her a toothy smile. "If you must bribe me for intel, I'd recommend wine and coffee."

Apparently, her intent had been obvious.

"Come on. You're following me. That means I'm in more danger here than Charles has told me. Can't blame a girl for wanting to know where she stands."

He made no reply.

"Did Charles find the source of the bounty on me?"

"I have no idea."

Chloe frowned. "Could you ask him? I mean, he sent you, right?"

She was grasping at straws.

"I'll try not to be offended by the assumption that someone like your Charles could order me around."

Chloe lifted a brow.

"He couldn't?"

"No."

He wasn't going to make her interrogation easy, was he?

"Then who did order you?"

He looked beyond her shoulder. "Your friends are looking for you."

Let them look for a second.

"It was Levi, right?"

She only knew two vampires. Well, given the fact that they'd met all of three times, she couldn't really say she knew Levi, but no one else came to mind.

The vampire narrowed his eyes.

"I'll take that as a yes. Why is he making you watch me?"

"You'd have to ask him."

Chloe sighed. Asking him wasn't a good idea. Being anywhere near Levi wasn't a good idea. She could have a perfectly civilized conversation—if a little pushy and nosy, perhaps—with just about anyone else, but she lost her mind around him.

"Yeah, right. I'll do that, I guess."

With a sigh, she started to walk away before turning back.

"Wait."

He hadn't yet dissolved into the shadows.

"What now?"

"What's your name?" she asked him. "If you're going to stalk me, we might as well get properly acquainted first."

He smiled. "Mikar."

"Did you call me on my first day, Mikar? To wake me up."

He shrugged. "You had orientation at ten."

Chloe managed a real smile. He might be intimidating and rather cold—she wasn't even going to start on the whole 'I only care if you get murdered a certain way' thing—but she was fairly certain he was the kind of person she wanted in her corner. If a random attacker leaped at her, Mikar would have him flat on his back in an instant.

She fell asleep a lot faster that night knowing she had someone watching over her.

But that didn't mean she wasn't extremely curious, and slightly irritated, as to Levi's reasons for hiring her a bodyguard to begin with. She knew she had to stay away. She didn't recognize herself around him. She didn't even recognize herself when she thought about him.

Who was she?

Quasi-reasonable

Time was flying at an alarming rate. One moment she was gaping at anything out of the ordinary, eyes widened all the way through Paranormal Intro and Immortal History, and then, somehow, she was used to it.

The elemental fights in the courtyard, the huntsmen kicking ass, the occasional shifter changing in the corridors, ravens coming to greet her between classes. Martie, the grumpy mailman. Fin, the strange Aos Si. The foxes, witches, wolves, and vampires—they were all part of her world now. She spent her Sunday mornings doing accounting for the huntsmen, studied every evening, and joined Jack's races whenever he called for one.

By the beginning of March, just three months after she'd first entered Oldcrest, it was her normal.

The one thing she hadn't yet learned to accept was the weather. The snow had melted—when Gwen wasn't playing with it, in any case—and the sky had been sunny for days, but it was still so cold Chloe mostly wore her coat, thermals, and two pairs of socks.

This week, a cold wind from the west had picked up, making her grumble every time she had to go outside.

She was yet again cursing the damn weather on her way from the dorms to the Institute when Jack called her.

"Hey, Cheetah. Ready for a prison break?"

Chloe grinned. She was really starting to like hanging out with Jack. She'd grown to understand why the huntsmen followed him. It was more than respecting him due to his rank, or even his mother's position; Jack had a way of making everything fun.

Case in point.

Chloe was comfortable in Oldcrest. She didn't freak out when Charles emailed her to say he didn't have any news about her attackers and might have to give up unless there was another development. She didn't care; here in the Institute, behind magic walls and around a thousand kick-ass sups, including one who was dedicated to her safety, she wasn't worried about some puny humans.

When Jack had first mentioned heading to London for a weekend, she'd immediately dismissed the idea. London was the daunting human place where Rose's Coven had been destroyed.

"I don't think I should go," she'd said.

The entire point of her being here was to avoid danger.

"Come on, Cheetah. It's gonna be a blast. Well, after we're done greeting Mom, in any case."

The huntsmen were heading south because the high guard would be in town.

Chloe had to admit, she was incredibly curious about the human woman who led a worldwide society of supernatural creature hunters, but she wasn't curious enough to leave Oldcrest. She loved the Institute so much she'd even toyed with the idea of asking Blair if she could try to become a teacher.

So she'd said no the first time, and Jack hadn't insisted.

He had, however, started to plan the trip, and everyone was talking about it. The boat ride along the Thames from London to Windsor, a castle tour, a quick trip to Brighton to surf and eat fish and chips on the beach.

Everyone was angling for an invitation; Chloe was one of the dozen people who had one, and she was wasting it because she was too much of a chicken to step out into the real world.

That was too sad for words.

After thinking things through, she called NOLA and mentioned her dilemma to Charles.

"Wait a minute. Some hunky huntsman, fully capable of taking out any human threat, offers to take you on a weekend trip to one of the hottest cities in the world, and you don't want to go?"

"I *do*," she corrected. "I'm just thinking that it might not be safe. And after all the effort you put in to get me here safely, it feels wrong to go out for fun."

"Honey, don't use me as an excuse to justify yourself. If you don't feel like pushing your boundaries? Don't. But if you're calling me to ask for permission, you got it."

She hadn't realized that was why she'd called. Because after he'd helped her get into the Institute for her safety, going on a pleasure trip Charles wouldn't have approved of seemed ungrateful. Disrespectful. But he didn't mind, so the next day, she asked Jack if she could still tag along.

The much-anticipated outing Jack had spent most of February organizing was happening this weekend. True to her nature, Blair had sent everyone tagging along a recommended list of stuff to pack, like they were a bunch of third-graders. Jack had looked at his list like it was a pit of snakes trying to bite him.

"Three pairs of underwear?" he'd asked.

"We're going from Friday evening to Monday. It seems appropriate," the witch replied with a bubbly smile.

"I don't wear underwear," Jack stated in response, answering the question everyone was probably asking themselves.

He wasn't a boxers *or* a briefs guy, apparently.

Chloe, for her part, had been rather glad of the list. She'd been thoroughly unprepared for her move from NOLA to Scotland, and, left to her own devices, she might not have thought to get a waterproof overcoat for the boat ride.

"I'm ready," she said to Jack, grinning. "We're leaving at three, right?"

He nodded. "Yeah, it's an eight-hour drive. Better get going early."

They'd decided to drive because flying wouldn't be easy with all the weapons they were carting around. Huntsmen were licensed to carry their axes, spears, bows, and swords, but going through customs was still a pain.

Chloe was taking one of the first driving shifts,

because she didn't quite feel comfortable enough to sit behind the wheel anywhere near a city; the endless empty Highland roads seemed safer, in case she slipped and ended up on the wrong side of the road.

She had some of her most fascinating lectures on Fridays, including Fin Varra's, but in her anticipation of the trip, she barely paid any attention, instead watching the clock that seemed to run a lot slower than usual. Finally, at two-thirty, she dashed out, heading back to the dorms to grab her things.

Gwen and Blair were already waiting in front of the dorm, the former with a duffle bag on the floor and the latter standing next to a hot pink suitcase.

"You guys are early!"

Gwen shook her head. "No, Jack asked us to set up some protective shields around the vans, just in case. He's bringing them over."

Lifting her head, Chloe could indeed see two large gray vehicles driving toward the dorm. To her surprise, they were coming from Night Hill.

Chloe's heart beat just a little faster, and she cursed herself.

Any acknowledgement of Oldcrest's middle hill never failed to tug her mind toward one of its inhabitants. And she knew that thinking of him at all was a terrible habit.

Levi De Villier.

She hadn't consciously thought about him in a while —during the day, at least. After their last meeting in his tower, she'd decided to stay the hell away from him. The way she acted around him wasn't normal, it wasn't her— and, in all honesty, it scared the shit out of her.

Chloe blamed the drop of witch blood in her veins.

That was the only explanation she had for these actions that went against her nature. So, she liked to pretend he didn't exist at all. It worked, most of the time. Oldcrest had enough distractions, and Levi stuck to his tower, his hill, his people.

She'd seen him a time or two in the distance. His unfair perfection struck her each time. So did her reaction to him. Her desire to get closer, to touch him, to practically climb into his skin.

"Right," she said, forcing her gaze away from the vans. "I'll take a shower and grab my bag; catch you in a few."

She ran up the stairs and rushed to her room.

Opening the door, Chloe froze.

He was here. Why was he here? He hadn't entered her room since January, although seven vials of sleeping draughts magically appeared on her nightstand once a week.

Levi was leaning on the beige and red wall, near the open window, next to Mikar.

She concentrated her attention on her stalker-bodyguard. Him, she could deal with.

The vampire was still following her, and Chloe was used to his shadow. He'd become a friend of sorts. Having him nearby was comforting.

"You know, I wish the thing about vampires not being able to enter places uninvited were true."

He laughed. "Sorry, child. Just following orders."

Dammit. Now she had to turn to Levi.

Chloe forced a smile. He definitely wasn't smiling back; instead, his expression was dark and dangerous. And incredibly alluring.

"Hi. Long time, no see."

"Oh, you've seen me," he replied. "You just like to pretend not to."

He'd noticed. Dammit.

"What can I help you with?"

A long second passed, then he talked, his tone even.

"It has come to our attention that you intend to leave the territory. Mikar will be accompanying you."

Chloe narrowed her eyes, blood boiling with a rage that she couldn't quite place.

"No."

A Bad Idea

She should have been grateful. She should have wept with relief. Had she not questioned her decision to leave out of fear? With Mikar by her side, she had no reason to be worried at all.

Chloe doubted that the huntsmen would pay attention to her at all times, but the vampire guard would keep his eye on her. This was a blessing.

But Levi was *telling* her what to do, and that ridiculous, childish, belligerent part of her that would not bend to him recoiled against the very notion.

Levi showed no surprise. The corner of his lips hiked up.

"That was a fact. I'm informing you as a courtesy. Mikar and Catherine have their orders and they will not break them."

Chloe willed herself to calm down and act like the reasonable woman she was. Thank you. The answer was yes, please, and thank you.

"Catherine?" she repeated.

Levi's smile grew broader, flashing teeth.

"Yes, Cat Stormhale. You might have seen her around; she studies biochemistry."

Chloe had seen her around. She was a beautiful, willowy loner who never gave anyone the time of day.

"I don't even know her; why would she want to babysit me?"

"She's the best-trained immortal currently available. If you want your pick of the guard, next time warn me before scheduling your little getaway."

Never mind being rational.

"Why would I? As it's apparently escaped your notice, I'm twenty-five, not six. And I don't answer to you, or anyone."

"I've noticed," he replied lightly. "Chloe, do you remember Primrose Hill? Do you want to know how close you were to being part of a murder scene—how those who took out nineteen fully trained witches left just an hour before you arrived?"

She blinked in shock. An hour? She'd planned to get there early. If the communal bathroom at the hostel where she'd crashed upon arriving in England hadn't been busy, she *might* have been there an hour earlier.

That notion made her sick to her stomach. She would have been, could have been, dead.

"I understand your nature will not allow you to submit to me," Levi said. He understood? That made one of them. "But you need to get it in your head that I'm not trying to dominate you. I'm trying to keep you safe."

Chloe *knew* he was protecting her.

She practically had to force the words out, but finally, she said, "Okay. I'll take Mikar and...Cat." It took more self-control, but finally, she also bit out, "Thank you."

To her surprise, Levi laughed. "I know how hard that was."

"Why?" she asked him. "Why can't I act normally around you? Are you using some sort of vampire mojo or something?"

Doubtful, but she would have liked to think so—because if he wasn't, that meant the problem really was her.

Levi glanced toward Mikar before answering. "Or something. It's a complicated question."

Now, at least, she had a reason to be pissed.

"Oh, come off it. Stop treating me like a damn kid and tell me! If there's something wrong with me, I need to know."

"There's nothing wrong with you," Mikar practically growled. "Nothing," he repeated, for emphasis.

She sighed. They didn't intend to tell her at all. Suddenly exhausted, she said, "Out. Both of you. Take the door, or window, or whatever. I need to take a shower and get ready. Until next time."

Mikar leaped onto the windowsill and jumped down. Levi remained. Of course he did.

"You'll have answers sooner than you think. And when you do, remember this: I'd bleed you now if I could."

Then, he was gone.

I'd bleed you now if I could.

She was right to mistrust him, right to be careful around him. But at the same time, he hadn't done anything to her, which meant that for whatever reason, he couldn't, and wouldn't hurt her.

For now.

Overall, Levi's appearance did end up helping. She

realized that she wasn't safe here in Oldcrest any more than she had been in NOLA. This was his domain, and although she felt strangely comfortable around him, he was saying he wanted to hurt her. He'd spelled it out to her practically each time they'd met.

He wanted to kill her. He hired a bodyguard to see that she was safe. He looked at her like she was dinner. He sent her sleeping draughts.

Nothing about Levi De Villier made sense. And under the hot stream of the shower jet, Chloe reminded herself that it didn't matter. He didn't matter. She liked her life here. She had friends aplenty, loved her lectures, and adored the food. He wasn't relevant.

He *wasn't*.

Chloe wasn't convincing anyone, let alone herself, but thankfully, she was quite gifted in the art of distracting her mind.

And she had a trip to London to look forward to.

They had two seven-seaters, and twelve of them were traveling, so they had two spare seats. Chloe hesitated at the door.

"Jack?" she called through the open window of the driver's seat. "Do you mind if a couple of people tag along?"

Feeling eyes on her, Chloe guessed Mikar and Cat were observing her from somewhere in the shadows— probably the Wolvswoods. She wasn't sure how they intended to travel south, but they might as well drive together. It was kinder on the environment, and besides, the huntsmen would probably notice vamps on their trail. Chloe didn't want to know what would happen if they ended up fighting each other.

Jack lifted a brow. "Sure, I guess. Who's that?"

She shrugged. "I heard there were vamps going to London this weekend."

His expression darkened dangerously. Jack was ripped, fast, and his every movement said predator, but before anything, he was a team leader. He even looked the part of a businessman or politician in his suits. Chloe had never been able to picture him as a huntsman.

Now, she could.

"I mean, I'm sure they can find their own way..."

"It's...fine. If there are suckers on the road, I'd rather have my eyes on them."

Now, she recalled him telling her during their trip to town last January with Tris that he wasn't fond of most vampires. Now she understood that might have been a euphemism. While Jack didn't have a problem with his cousin, despite her being a fledgling, he seemed to *hate* vampires.

She wished she could take the words back, but a breathtakingly beautiful blonde with long wavy hair stepped out of the woods, Mikar by her side.

"Joy," she said, with the most unfriendly, fake smile Chloe had ever seen. "Riding with blood bags."

Oh dear.

An Engrossing Tale

A terrible idea didn't cover it.

"So, you're huntsmen in training, is that right?" Cat asked, batting her long lashes.

"Fully trained huntsmen," Bash amended. "We're in the Institute because furthering our education serves the order."

"I see. So, you've all murdered immortals and other sups already. Good to know."

Jack had closed the window and put the heating on, but the air in the car was ice anyway.

"Can we ride with Tris instead?" Gwen whispered to Chloe.

Cat's bright green eyes turned to the back seat where Chloe was huddled between Gwen and Mikar.

"And you're a witch," she said to Gwen. "Unusual, wouldn't you say, for one of you to spend time with huntsmen? You know they're behind most of the witch massacres throughout history?"

Blair, seated beside Cat in the second row, replied, "Actually, that was mostly regular human men killing random regular human women for kicks. Trust me, I'm from the Salem Coven. We know our history. Huntsmen and witches have a great relationship where I'm from in the States. They come to us for protective spells; we go to them when we have a rogue shifter problem, or whatever."

Cat all but hissed.

"Ignore her," Mikar told them. "Catherine is a Stormhale. Her family's storm magic is unpredictable. They've made a mess a billion times throughout history, and huntsmen have had to put down too many of her people. She isn't objective."

"Stormhale," Chloe echoed.

Levi had mentioned that name, but now she thought of it, she'd heard it before then.

One of the seven, she realized. The seven families directly changed by Ariadne, the vampires' creator. Blair had called them vampire royalty.

Suddenly remembering that frustrating conversation from three months ago, Chloe asked, "Hey, what are the founding families again? De Villier, Drake, Stormhale, Helsing..."

Cat didn't miss a beat, finishing the list for her.

"Beauforts, Rosedean, and Eirikrson."

Eirikrson. That was it. The one Blair had refused to talk about.

Chloe felt like the name was familiar to her, some-how, although she'd be hard-pressed to say where she'd heard it.

Eirikrson...

"It must be amazing to come from a line with so much history," Gwen said.

Cat turned to her and smiled, completely changing

her features. She no longer seemed quite so cold or unfriendly. She looked younger and, if anything, more beautiful.

"We have stories that go back to the Roman times. You wouldn't believe half of it. And don't get me started with the family heirlooms." She winked at Gwen. "Jewels. Loads and loads of jewels."

Reiss laughed at her side. "I bet. Shame no one can get into the Eirikrson coffers. There must be so many treasures lying around in their dusty old mansion."

Cat visibly relaxed. "In Rome, we have a painting of my great-aunt with Liz Eirikrson. Her sword had a diamond the size of a fist, she wore the most gorgeous ruby necklace, and don't get me started on her diadem. To know that they're all lying over there, unappreciated, breaks my heart."

Chloe could feel Mikar stiffen. They were approaching a subject most people didn't want to talk about—to her, in any case. But Reiss and Cat, at least, hadn't received the memo. They talked without filter.

"Why are they unappreciated?" Chloe pushed.

Cat shrugged. "All the Eirikrsons are dead, save for the crazy one guarded in Oldcrest. And while their servants who are still alive do have access to Skyhall, the house atop Night Hill, they refuse to do anything with their fortune. Such a waste."

"They don't *refuse* to do anything," Bash protested. "I hear that their treasures are sealed under a blood lock. No one can get in their coffer, except an Eirikrson."

"Maybe," Cat muttered. "My mom thinks the Eirikrson's slayers are just saying that so they can keep everything to themselves. Who knows?"

"Did you say one of them still lives in Oldcrest? Couldn't he claim it?"

The car fell silent. Absolutely silent. Then, everyone laughed—even Jack, who'd been tense for the last hour. The one exception was Mikar, whose jaw was tight. He didn't like the turn of conversation.

"She's a regular," said Gwen, as an explanation, or an apology; Chloe couldn't quite tell. "I didn't realize no one had told you about Oldcrest. I would have, if I'd known."

After three months, she'd mostly stopped feeling like a newbie who didn't understand sup basics. Then came moments like this.

"Thousands of years ago, the territory was shielded by one of the most powerful witches this world has ever known," Cat said. "The wards make the entire place invisible to all of those who haven't been invited, regular or sups alike, and that's in order to keep that guy locked tight. The seven families moved onto Night Hill, and it was declared that one of them would live here and stand guard every year. It's the one thing the seven have ever agreed on: that Eirikr needs to stay locked up. He was insane. Killed every vampire who wasn't part of his family. All of the other families were in hiding because of him. And he wanted to murder Ariadne, too."

Chloe blinked in surprise. The story made no sense.

"He wants to murder a goddess?"

"It's technically possible. Gods are immortal, not eternal. Cut their head, stop their heart, and they're gone, just like you or me. But it generally takes a god to kill a god. The thing is, Eirikr was almost as powerful as the gods themselves. There were rumors saying that, as we're made of her blood, if she died, we'd all die with her. So, we decided it was safer to keep him locked up and throw away the key."

Suddenly, Chloe felt a wind around her hair, although the car was still locked up. She remembered the trail on Coscnoc, beyond the black tape. The darkening, twisted path calling to her.

"That man," she said, her throat dry. "That vampire... he's on the east hill, right?"

"Yeah, in a cave, protected by so many spells your head will spin just going anywhere near it. He's been there for a long time. Don't worry about him."

"Hey, there's a resting area right ahead. You wanna stretch your legs?" Mikar asked.

"Sure thing."

That was the end of the conversation. Next, they talked music, and then movies, followed by the difficulties of beheading someone with a thick neck. Cat seemed to warm up to the others in light of their common interests—particularly the beheading.

But Chloe's mind remained on the hill. The trail.

And the creature within.

A Portrait

They arrived in London in the middle of the night and headed to an overpriced parking garage.

They'd stopped several times, but after close to ten hours on the road with bad traffic, Chloe's every limb was stiff and uncomfortable. She stretched next to the car while the others grabbed their bags.

"So, who are you?"

Chloe looked up to find Cat standing right next to her, arms folded on her chest, eyes fixed on her.

"He doesn't talk to me or acknowledge my existence for three months, then the Leviathan tells me to follow your ass to London. And you're a regular," she added, making air quotes around the last word with her fingers. "I don't buy it."

Chloe shrugged. "Trust me, I'd love to be a cool creature—or a vampire princess like you. But I'm just...me."

"You don't feel like a regular," Cat stated.

Chloe had heard that enough times. "Thanks, I

guess? But I am. The queen of NOLA's coven tested my blood. It's normal."

"What did she test?" Cat questioned.

Chloe tilted her head. "I don't know? That it was normal, or something. She thinks I probably had some witch ancestry because my blood responds to her magic a little, but that's about it."

Cat wasn't the only one paying attention. Both Mikar and Jack had walked closer. Chloe bit her lip, self-conscious.

"But," she said, "other than that, I'm normal."

Chloe could tell that Cat was skeptical. She tried not to find it irritating, and failed. Didn't the vamp princess think that Chloe would have liked to be one of them?

"Hey, Cheetah, is that your bag?"

Bash pulled her backpack out of the boot. Chloe smiled as she took it from him, knowing he'd just given her a way out of the conversation.

"Thanks."

"Any time, girl."

Those huntsmen really were a nice bunch. Even if they had decimated Cat's ancestors.

"All right, listen up," Jack said. "Outside, we're not supposed to draw attention to ourselves. Fourteen people stand out. We'll walk in groups of three to four at all times. I, Tris, Bash, and Reiss know all of the London safe houses, so make sure you're always close to one of us. Writing the address anywhere isn't an option. No weapons in the street if we can avoid it—the last thing we need is bad press." He marked a pause. "We have a target on our backs at all times. Most sups can't stand us because they know if they step out of line, we're the ones who'll come calling. They can feel us, smell us, and they might cause trouble. We have two witches and one regular with us." He now gestured to Gwen, Blair, and Chloe. "No trouble permitted on this trip, got it?"

The huntsmen nodded their agreement before setting out into the cool air.

It was warmer than it had been in January, according to the temperature displayed on her phone, but a cold sixty-mile-per-hour wind negated that, chilling her to the bone although she was wearing her coat. Chloe wished she had gloves, a scarf, thermals under her jeans, earmuffs, a hat, and...

She stopped at the sight of a perfectly manicured hand outstretched in front of her.

Cat was handing her what looked like expensive leather gloves.

Chloe looked up to the stunning creature. Cat shrugged. "I don't get cold," she said. Realizing it wasn't much of an explanation, she added, "Your clacking teeth are irritating."

She gratefully took the gloves. They were lined with wool.

"Oh, Cat, they're wonderful."

The vampire was already storming forward, ten paces away.

Social, she was not. But Cat was obviously very thoughtful.

"Don't trust her."

Chloe turned, finding Mikar right behind her.

"Why?"

He was glaring at the woman.

"She's a Stormhale, for one. Your friend wasn't wrong. They're known to be unstable. They were a clan of powerful witches before they were turned by Ariadne.

That's too much strength in one family. The vamp folks out in the world don't quite understand—they see the seven as their betters, their nobility. No one gets that there's a clear hierarchy. For a long time, our kind deferred to the seven in one specific order—Eirikrsons, De Villiers, Drakes, Stormhales, then the rest, quibbling over the base of the pyramid. The De Villiers are spread throughout the world. The Drakes are low in numbers, relying on their own strength. It was the Stormhales who started the coup that dethroned the Eirikrsons. Now she turns up, trying to get her claws in Levi...it's not good news. She may obey Levi's orders for now, but she only answers to the head of her family."

Chloe's head was going to spin. She looked down at her hands. The gloves had been cold inside a moment ago, but now they were starting to warm up.

"It sounds like vampire problems. Vampire politics. If she's nice to me, I'll be nice back."

She was generally cool with everyone, whether or not they proved to be kind first.

"It is *your* problem," Mikar retorted. "Levi has ordered her to watch you. She's already questioned why. If Catherine thinks you're Levi's plaything, and that having you is the reason why he isn't interested in her— well." Mikar looked up to the city sky. Barely any stars were visible here; the lights of London clouded them. "It looks like a storm is coming. And accidents happen. A bolt of lightning conveniently hitting a tree right next to you..."

Chloe glared at Mikar. "You know, I have a very low tolerance for bullshit. Since the beginning of time, men have encouraged women to mistrust each other, see each other as rivals. Guess what? If she wants that control freak, she can have him. I'm certainly not calling dibs."

Mikar laughed. "All right. Just be careful."

Chloe decided to ignore every single thing she just heard. Her hands were warm. That was the only fact worth remembering.

They turned off Oxford Circus, and then turned again a few times into identical white square rows of houses that made Chloe understand why Jack had warned them to stay with those who knew the way. She noted a Victoria's Secret, Louis Vuitton, and a charming little park. At least if she got lost, she could return to the general area.

Her group, led by Bash, arrived in front of a house so very similar to Rose's Coven that Chloe's heart skipped a beat.

But there was no body, no smell of blood. As Bash walked up the steps to the door, Jack opened it from the inside.

"Come on in. I've made tea."

Chloe practically ran up the stairs.

She'd never liked coffee. Tea was better, although she still didn't quite get why the Brits were so obsessed with it. But right now, she would have drunk just about anything, provided it was served warm.

Inside, the walls were painted dark green and hung with paintings that seemed both old and masterful, the sort of art one saw in museums. But instead of a pretty smiling lady or a Romanesque couple walking through a park, the portraits depicted men and women armed with weapons, scenes of battles against demons. The huntsmen had their own history.

"You like?" Jack asked, seeing her pause in front of an oil painting.

A vampire, if she wasn't mistaken. A very handsome man with silver hair and bright blue eyes. His fangs weren't extended, but the painter had ensured that the light on his skin was luminous, unnatural.

"Who is this?" she asked. "It's strange to see a vamp here."

"Strange if you don't know our history, I guess. This is Eirikr. The guy the others were talking about in the car."

Chloe was startled and confused. "But they said he was insane and murderous."

"That's one point of view," Jack replied, chuckling. "Eirikr was hell-bent on eradicating vampires who drank human blood and killed their victims. In his days, that was almost every vamp. Now, they have synthetic blood —and besides, they've learned to control their thirst, evolutionarily-speaking. Back then...it wasn't pretty." Jack's jaw was set. "Eirikr founded the huntsmen."

Now, her jaw hit the floor. "Seriously?"

Jack smiled. "He trained a bunch of humans person-ally. Those who were strong enough, fast enough, he changed. He had a witch with him; one drop of his blood, a hell of a lot of magic, and here we are. He only used a very small dose of his own blood to ensure we wouldn't turn. But it's here, in our veins. It's been passed down through every generation of huntsmen, hence why we have a chance against sups."

The more she heard about their founder, she more intrigued she was. Eirikr sounded complicated. But also something else. Not mad, or cruel. Passionate. Purposeful.

"So you're part vamp," she teased him.

Jack grimaced. "I'm part Eirikrson. Different."

Suddenly curious, Chloe asked, "What about the coffers? Cat says only an Eirikrson could get to them. Have you guys tried?"

Jack shook his head. "No. We have no interest in his wealth. He provided us with plenty of heirlooms, anyway. If we had any control over what happens in Oldcrest...let's just say Eirikr wouldn't be rotting in a cave."

Though his tone was light, Chloe was starting to understand the divide between huntsmen and vampires. The reason behind the unfriendliness, the tension.

The land she loved was a divided faction that could easily turn into a battlefield.

"Let's get that tea, shall we?" Jack said lightly. "I think there might be some chocolate in the cupboard if you prefer."

The man was starting to know her well.

Blood and Cashmere

CHAPTER

C hloe woke to find a folded package on her bed. She opened it, and inside was a checked scarf with white, blue, and baby pink lines. It was so warm and soft.

The package wasn't signed. Chloe sighed. When would she cease to seem so pathetic to her friends that they bought her expensive stuff? It wasn't like she couldn't afford to clothe herself, especially now that she'd worked as an accountant for three months. She didn't spend much in Oldcrest, so most of her salary was sitting nicely in her bank account, waiting to be spent.

Maybe whoever had bought it would let her pay them back; then she could keep it. It was so pretty, she would be loath to part with it.

Her bladder demanding her attention, Chloe dropped the fabric back on the bed and got up.

The tall three-story house had several small bedrooms to house huntsmen as they traveled to London. No en-suite. She peeked out the door and, finding the corridors empty, dashed to claim the bathroom on her floor. She didn't stay long under the hot shower, knowing all twelve of them had to share one boiler. After her ablutions, she got dressed, then put on her leather boots and her coat, along with Cat's gloves.

Then Chloe glanced at the scarf. Recognizing the label, she shivered, wondering how much it had cost—and who had spent that sort of money on her. Her mind went to Levi, but he was all the way up in Scotland. That left everyone else here.

She took the scarf with her downstairs. A delicious smell was beckoning her to a large formal dining room.

Bacon. There was bacon in the air.

She stopped as she got to the door, finding a lot more people than she'd expected.

In addition to the nine huntsmen and her two witch friends—the vampires were patrolling somewhere outside; they hadn't come inside the previous evening—there were new faces.

They all seemed beautiful to her, like big-screen actors or models. There was one plump woman playing with a dagger. Her pink cherry mouth and strawberry hair said soft and sweet, but her dexterity with sharp objects proved that to be a lie. There was also a tall woman with short dark hair, and another shorter one perched on a chest of drawers. The three others were guards, judging by the way they held themselves stiffly and stood close to the exits.

"Well, well." The short woman's gaze was intense. "What have we here?"

"Another friend," Jack replied lightly.

Chloe hadn't noticed at first, but now it was clear that the woman was related to Jack. She had his nose, his eyes, and his aura. Everything about her said leader.

His mother. The high guard.

Damn, good genes ran in the family. She didn't seem to be a day over thirty, if that.

The vampire blood, Chloe guessed.

"Friend, hm?" She winked at her son. "Whatever you say. Just hurry and make pretty babies, will you?"

Jack groaned. Tris seemed to be on cloud nine.

The woman waved to Chloe, then pointed to her own chest. "Becca Hunter."

"Chloe Miller," she replied.

Becca pointed to the table. "Come. Sit. Eat."

Orders. Chloe knew she would have hissed and made a point of standing until she grew roots if they'd come from Levi, but the friendly woman's tone didn't bother her. Plus, there was bacon.

She sat down, and Blair passed her a plate of eggs.

Various trays filled the table—mushrooms, bread rolls, roasted tomatoes, sausages, mash, and bacon. So much bacon.

She piled the food onto her plate. Before digging in, she remembered the scarf. Chloe lifted it in the air.

"I found this on my bed. Who bought it for me?"

Silence. "On your bed?" Jack repeated.

Chloe nodded. "It wasn't there last night. It was in a box. No note or anything. I thought it might be from Cat or Mikar..."

"Call them. Check," he said, reaching for the scarf.

But the moment Jack's hand touched the fabric, the scarf moved of its own volition, crawling quickly up the side of Chloe's arms, tightening at each revolution. It was slithering to her neck, she realized, frozen in fear. Her arm was growing more and more painful with each passing instant as it squeezed hard enough to break bone, stopping her blood circulation.

And then, a sharp pain cut through the numbness. One of the three older female huntsmen—the redhead —had cut through the fabric. Chloe's blood ran onto her shoulder, red and dizzying.

The lovely scarf was in pieces on the floor.

"Don't touch that," Becca ordered her son, who was bending down toward what was left of it. "The spell might not be broken yet."

Jack nodded, pulling a knife out of his jacket. Did everyone have a knife? And why didn't she?

Chloe chuckled. She could count on her strange brain to think of the most stupidly inappropriate response to almost being strangled by a scarf.

"You're okay?" Gwen whispered.

Chloe nodded, with difficulty. Becca said, "Your friend is probably in shock. Do you have a spell for that?"

Gwen shook her head, but Blair was already pulling a flask out of her bag. "Two drops," she told Chloe, who opened the bottle and drank it without question.

Almost immediately, warmth spread through her— she hadn't even realized she was so cold. Her trembling fingers went still. She breathed out.

"That was awesome. Greer Vespian again?" Chloe asked.

Blair beamed. "I take it for anxiety—one drop per day. Two is for shock, and three is in case of paralysis."

Someone ought to sell GP's potions worldwide. She'd put pharma firms out of business in no time.

Chloe's full attention returned to the huntsmen, who

were examining the piece of scarf on the tip of Jack's knife.

"It's clearly elemental magic. An air mage, I'd say."

"Could be. Or blood magic. Hard to tell, now that it's not active. We'll have to take it to the lab."

"Maybe we should stop thinking about what it is and start wondering how it got inside one of our safe houses, and why it targeted the girl," one of the male guards said.

Becca lifted her head toward him and grinned.

"See, boy?" she told Jack. "Always marry someone smarter than you."

The guard rolled his eyes.

Chloe hadn't paid him or the two others much mind, but now she could tell—the dark blonde hair, tall stature, handsome mouth. This was Jack's father. Or his clone, one of the two. They really looked alike. Chloe wanted to ask Jack to stand next to him so she could compare the two specimens. She doubted she'd find more than a handful of differences.

Becca's attention returned to Chloe.

"You're a guest in our home. This should never have happened, and will not happen again. Now, who have you pissed off?"

A question she would have preferred not to answer. Ever.

"Me? No one. Not pissing off people is my hobby, really. I'm nice."

She'd made a point of that.

The leader of the huntsmen looked like she was about to call bullshit.

"But I'm the daughter of a serial killer. The families of his victims...let's just say they aren't very fond of me."

Chloe didn't look at her friends, eyes on her finger-tips. She didn't want to see their expressions change. Read judgment.

But it had to be said, because if George's antics had something to do with the strangling scarf, they needed to know, but damn if she didn't hate talking about it.

Becca frowned. "I guess they could have hired a witch, but it's doubtful. To risk pissing *us* off, whoever snuck in here has a clear personal stake in this. Jack, you will watch your friend's back, personally."

Chloe blushed. "No need, I have two guards. Cat and Mikar. They're..."

"The vamps. That's why you wanted them to travel with us." Jack groaned, frustrated. "A little warning next time, Cheetah?"

Now she was getting pissed. "I didn't know they'd do anything here, okay? The people after me are in the States. And until now, they've only been regular humans."

The full scale of the situation hit her now. She had witches after her. Witches. Creatures who could stop her heart or make her bleed out or worse.

No amount of GV potions could help with that fact. She was a dead woman walking.

"All right, we'll get to the bottom of this, but for now, shields. Mental, physical, and a warning bell too."

Blair leaped to her feet.

"I can help."

Becca laughed.

"Oh no. Witch magic is strong, but it dies with the caster and often grows weaker as days go by."

"Then what..."

Becca's husband, who'd been near the door a moment ago, was now kneeling in front of Chloe.

He wore a long black coat, gloves, boots—every part of him was covered, save for his handsome face.

When he removed his gloves, Chloe gasped. Except for his face, every visible inch of skin was covered with intricate marks that seemed to glow—dark silvery-steel tattoos flowing like water on his flesh.

"What are you?" she asked him.

Not the politest of questions. She really ought to work on that loose tongue of hers.

He didn't seem to mind.

"A god," he replied simply. "Your hands."

Chloe looked up to Jack. "What does that make you?"

"A freak," Tris said under her breath.

Jack laughed. "A scion, I guess. Kind of? Dad is a pretty weak god, though. So, I'm just a huntsman."

Chloe gave her hands to the man, who closed his eyes and smiled. "There's a lot more than meets the eye in you, isn't there, Chloe?"

She froze.

"Yes. It has been an age since one of you has risen. I wonder..." He glanced at his wife. "But no matter. For now, let us just ensure you keep breathing."

Warmth spread through his fingers, heating up every part of her.

"It might get a little uncomfortable, but it won't last," he told her softly.

She bit her lip and winced. The heat was getting hotter and hotter, boiling her insides. What was he doing to her?

For a wild second, she wondered if he was hurting

her, trying to kill her; maybe he was the one who'd given her the scarf.

But the next moment, it stopped. Blair gasped. "Was that a transfusion?"

Chloe had no clue what that meant, but the god nodded.

"Dad has some nanocytes inside his body," Jack said. "Incredibly advanced stuff, light years ahead of anything created on Earth. They've evolved alongside him, are a part of him. That's how those humans called gods are so strong, and seemingly immortal. There are billions of nanoparticles inside him. Think of them as little computers with artificial intelligence. He's ordered a few of them to go inside you. They aren't made for you, so they'll die eventually—unless he takes them back. But while they're inside you, they'll protect you, improve your endurance, that sort of thing."

"And they'll let me know if you're in danger," the god added. "Consider yourself officially under the protection of the huntsmen. For now."

Alive

C hloe shut off the little voice that wanted her to head right back under the blankets upstairs after that thing had squeezed her, trying to claim her life.

She was in London. She was around huntsmen, who would now be a lot more vigilant about what was going on around her. There were two vampires watching her. She was not going to let some cowardly witch asshole ruin her trip—or her friends'. Besides, her room was clearly no safer than anywhere else.

Though her appetite had disappeared, she forced a few bites of everything on her plate and made a point of smiling a lot, joining everyone's conversations. By the end of breakfast, her face felt like it was going to split in two. Her throat was dry and overworked. She had never noticed how much effort talking and smiling took.

They cleared their plates and gathered in the hallway. Before she left the kitchen, Bash pulled her sleeve.

"Stop."

She frowned at him.

"We get it. This morning sucks. Stop trying to fake having fun for our sakes. It's not working, and it'll only make you more miserable. You smile when you want to, got it?"

She did smile at him then—her first real one since the scarf. "All right."

Outside, both Mikar and Cat were waiting on the pavement, a frown in place.

"Something's wrong."

Chloe wondered how they could tell.

"Someone got into my room and gave me a scarf that tried to strangle me."

The two vampires glanced at each other.

"A scarf?"

To her relief, Blair explained the events of breakfast. Mikar never stopped glowering as he listened.

"Someone got into your room...and just dropped a scarf on the bed. That doesn't add up."

"No one got near the house last night," Cat added, somewhat defensively.

She wanted it understood she'd done her job right.

"I know. Thank you so much for watching me, Catherine, Mikar."

She hadn't said that to them yet.

The vamp relaxed while Mikar walked away, phone in hand. To report to his boss, Chloe guessed.

Chloe was pretty certain that if he'd appeared right then, she would have been fully capable of expressing the extent of her gratitude. She did need her guards. She was powerless.

How many times had they helped her without her knowing it? Had they prevented attacks in Oldcrest?

She wanted—needed—to know. She daren't ask.

"Right. Who's up for a boat ride?"

CHLOE YET AGAIN PROVED THAT HER STRONGEST SKILL was distracting herself. Out on the water, wind on her face, she didn't even care about the cold. Which might have had a lot to do with the fact that the cruise day included afternoon tea and unlimited champagne top-up.

Afternoon tea, she learned, was an adorable British custom that involved mini sandwiches and cakes on tiered plate stands. She went back for at least five three-inch-tall Victoria sponges and two serving of scones with jam and clotted cream. To crown a wonderful day, her bright yellow waterproof overcoat was doing its job, keeping her mostly dry.

By the early evening, when they were back in the London docks, she had messy hair and a light heart.

She hoped she'd remember this day. Her friends, the food, the boat. The scarf was a bleep on the radar.

"You're so strong. A lot stronger than me. I'd be in pieces, if I were you," Blair said.

Chloe shrugged.

"I'm just used to life getting in the way of happiness. So I learned to enjoy the moments and be grateful for them."

The witch watched her before smiling. "We should toast. To the moment."

Chloe laughed. "We've toasted plenty, thank you."

She'd never liked getting drunk; Chloe was one to stop halfway to tipsy.

She soon realized she was the exception among her

group, besides Jack, who only had one flute of champagne and, hours later, at dinner, sipped on red wine,
taking his time. But the others were downing their
drinks like water.

Jack's advice on staying inconspicuous and traveling
separately long forgotten, their group wobbled through
Mayfair, singing and dancing on the pavement.

"Don't look so disapproving," Jack said with a laugh.
"They can take a nest of rogue shifters while half-drunk.
It's actually part of the training."

Of course it was.

"I'm not disapproving. I just don't understand the
desire to lose control."

Jack nodded as they turned into New Bond Street.
During the day, the street was a hub of activity, with
black taxis driving over the speed limit; now, it was
empty. "You wouldn't," he said, understanding in his
tone. "Those who've had the rug pulled from under their
feet rarely do. What happened with your dad...I'm sorry.
It sucks. But it doesn't define you."

Didn't it?

"It's hard to believe that when I'm basically on the
run, in another continent, because of it. I had to give up
my home, move, and now..."

Jack was thoughtful. "You're assuming that this mess
has something to do with your father. It's possible..."

He never finished that sentence.

A spear flashed through the air, aimed right at his
head. The next instant, unbelievably, Jack moved a fraction of an inch to the left and caught it in motion.

"In formation!" he yelled.

The huntsmen, who'd barely seemed able to walk on
a straight line moments before, moved as one, forming a

circle back-to-back with Chloe, Blair, and Gwen in the middle.

It looked like they'd be putting that drunken training to the test.

The seconds were thick, heavy, endless. Nothing happened. After a minute, Chloe wondered if it had just been a huntsmen-hating prank, someone seeing an opportunity to try and hurt Jack.

But in the next instant, both sides of the long, wide street darkened as a crowd of yelling, growling creatures ran right to them.

The creatures were armed with spears and swords, and some had guns. Chloe couldn't quell her fear. So many of them. Dozens. Perhaps a hundred. She couldn't tell in the dark.

To her left, Blair lifted her hands to shoulder height and yelled. Bright light flashed out of her palms and flew through the thick crowd of enemies, knocking a good few over. Gwen's eyes were on the sky. Her dark irises flashed silver-white, and the sky thundered in response to her call. Fist-size balls of ice fell from the sky, hitting everyone outside of their circle.

Everyone was useful except her.

Chloe wasn't one to enjoy violence. Other than for self-defense, she'd never been interested in fighting. She'd always thought that violence only bred more violence in an unending circle of animosity.

Right now, she felt foolish. Downright foolish. Those creatures weren't going to stop just because she didn't want to fight. They didn't care. They'd planned this ambush to destroy every single one of them. And Chloe should have been able to fight or, at the very least, defend herself and be useful to her friends.

She saw one of Tris's many spare blades flash at her belt.

"Can I have a knife?" she asked her.

Without sparing her a glance, Tris pulled a long, curved knife out of her jacket and threw it behind her.

Chloe's fingers wrapped around the hilt, grabbing it like a lifeline. At least now she didn't feel so very useless.

The creatures were almost on them, close enough for her to see that their faces seemed wrong, contorted into a mask of hunger and horror. What were they?

The first line reached the huntsmen, and blades fell on blades in a thundering clash with such speed that Chloe could barely follow the movements.

The things had sharp, vampire-like teeth, though much longer than any vamp's fangs Chloe had ever seen. And it wasn't just their canines—at least four, and sometimes even eight, of their teeth protruded from their mouths.

They didn't have the strength, but they had the numbers. Chloe saw one fallen creature crawling on the floor, mouth wide open to bite Bash. She screamed, "Watch out!" and ran to her friend.

Too afraid to give much thought to her actions, she plunged her knife deep inside the creature's skull before its jaw closed on him.

That was when she realized she could be helpful. The huntsmen were protecting her and the witches, and she could protect them by looking around and defending them from sneaky attacks.

She concentrated on that job, awkwardly pushing her knife through legs, over shoulders, and under arms.

She would have sworn that a lifetime had passed, but Mikar appeared only minutes later, Cat by his side.

Something changed in the air. Chloe could almost taste fear. The moment the creatures saw them, they attempted a retreat. And she understood why.

Mikar had never seemed threatening to her until then. He was certainly muscular, and there was an edge to his dark eyes. But she'd never stopped to think what he'd done to earn himself a place as one of Levi's guards.

Now she knew she was facing a killer. The sort of man who took lives with ease, perhaps even pleasure. At his side, Cat was a tigress. A cat ready to pounce and play with her food.

The creatures never had a chance.

Chloe saw nothing more than shadows in the wind. Claws flashing and blood pouring out of ripped throats. She'd been impressed by Gwen's hail, but Cat's hands propelled thunder that destroyed everything in its path.

An instant later, all but one of the creatures were in pieces on the ground, and the street was silent and motionless. Then, as if freaked by the atmosphere, a nearby car alarm rang out.

Tris laughed. She *laughed*.

And the next moment, Chloe was laughing too.

Everything *was* hilarious.

They were alive.

A Conversation

"Let's get out of here now," Mikar said, walking quickly toward the huntsmen's quarters. "This is bad news. Has anyone been bitten?" There were noes all around.

"Good. Let's go in."

"What were those things?" Chloe asked.

"Ferals. Vampires affected by a blood sickness that makes them insane. They're insatiable and incapable of thinking very much. Seeing this many in one place can only mean one thing: they were ordered here. Spelled, or mind controlled. *Faster*," Mikar admonished, although they were already practically jogging.

He was really freaked out, she could tell. Chloe quickened her pace, and in no time, they'd arrived in front of the huntsmen's house.

Jack stopped in front of Mikar, sizing him up. His jaw tight, he said, "You helped tonight."

Mikar gave no reply.

"I know you were told to protect her, but you helped us too. You may stay with us if you'd like. Both of you."

The vampires looked taken aback. Chloe guessed they weren't often invited inside huntsmen's quarters.

"Appreciated. But someone has to watch the house from the outside."

"Chloe was attacked inside, too," Cat argued. "I'll stay with her. If that's all right with you," she added, to no one in particular.

Mikar looked like it definitely wasn't all right with him. Before he could protest, Chloe said, "Sounds great. Thank you. After last night, I'll sleep better with you here."

Reluctantly, the other vampire nodded. "All right. I'll call Levi with an update."

That was either a warning or a reminder for Cat, Chloe guessed. She shot a glare at Mikar. She'd never judge someone because of their family—not after what had happened with her father.

"Wait a minute," Jack called to Mikar as he retreated. "Bounty hunters, witches, and now feral vamps all going for Chloe? And you guys, the upper crust of vampire society, watching her back? If we hadn't been here, she would have been dead by the time you arrived. If we're her first line of defense, we need to know what's going on. So we can be prepared."

Chloe already knew Mikar's answer before he said it. "I don't have the clearance to get into it. Let's just get through this trip. Then I will personally ask Levi to bring you up to speed." He swept all of them in one glance. "All of you."

Her included, then.

She held on to that.

The night wasn't nearly as bad as it could have been, partially because Blair was traveling with the entirety of the GV catalogue in her bag, which included a sleeping draught almost as efficient as Alexius's, and partially because Cat was sleeping in the next room. After seeing her in action, Chloe had never felt safer.

She woke up to her phone vibrating on her bedside table. Chloe looked at the screen and frowned in confusion. Not only was the call coming from an unknown number, but it was also requesting a video feed.

Yawning, she pressed the green button. If the caller turned out to be a creep, hanging up would be easy enough.

On the screen, an all too familiar face wearing a smug grin appeared. She groaned.

"Did I wake you up?"

"It's..." She glanced at the time on her phone. "Six in the morning on a Sunday, so yes."

"My apologies."

Why did everything he say sound so sarcastic? To her surprise, she didn't feel the need to push, irritate, and question everything he said today.

"I hear you've had quite the trip so far."

He said it carefully, as if wondering whether mentioning her trials might make her break. But she wasn't breaking. She wasn't afraid—not anymore. Fear had given way to determination.

Chloe didn't know what made her tell him, but she said, "I want to train. I want to be able to hold my own if something like that happens again. I don't want to freeze or feel hopeless."

If he'd laughed, she might have truly hated him. But Levi's smile broadened.

"Excellent," he said.

"And I want you to tell me who's after me. And why. It makes no sense. It's not about my dad, is it?"

The human attackers in NOLA had made sense. But the magic and the feral vampires really didn't.

"And don't just threaten to kill me to shut me up. I know you won't."

"You've never been more mistaken," Levi said, a hint of fangs flashing. "I'll tell you who's after you—if only so you know what you're up against. The reason why isn't something I will divulge quite yet."

That was something—a huge leap compared to where they'd been just two days ago.

"Well?"

His grin disappeared. "You've been told about the seven, the families that rule our kind. While those behind the attacks on you have done their best to remain in the shadows, it is quite clear that they have resources. The power to control ferals, the money to hire bounty hunters. At first, they were human, and if that scheme had worked out, no one would have suspected the source of the attack. But Mikar and the rest of my guard have stopped over a dozen killers—some well-renowned and expensive."

The truth was even worse than her suspicions.

"Not many have the power to go to those lengths. I fear you're targeted by one of us. A royal. An old and powerful creature."

"But why?" she asked, almost pleading.

Levi hesitated. "An interesting question. Some among our kind can see the future. Perhaps you may become a threat to our kind someday."

Definitely not what she'd imagined.

"That literally makes no sense. I'm just...me."

Chloe Miller. Twenty-Five. Good with numbers and with ravens. Unless he was hiding money and she ended up figuring it out while working for the taxman, she didn't see how she could ever threaten an ancient vampire.

"I'm just human."

"So were the creatures that cornered you yesterday. Once, long ago, they were just human."

Chloe winced. "You're saying I could become gross and crazy."

"I'm saying some people evolve."

She wasn't quite done with him yet.

"So why are you helping me if I could be dangerous?" She couldn't say that with a straight face.

Levi laughed. "You asked. I answered. I never promised explanations."

She glared. "You're incredibly irritating, you know that?"

Levi held his hands to his heart, pretending to be hurt. "It wounds me. Truly."

She had to roll her eyes.

"Are you coming back today?" he asked her.

She nodded. "That's the plan."

"Good. Training tonight. On the hill."

Chloe opened her mouth, then closed it again. "No, I meant I'd train with...Jack. Or Mikar. Or maybe I could ask Professor Anika."

Literally anyone but him.

He grinned. "Oh no, fledgling. You'll train with the only one who can prepare you to face an ancient vampire. Me."

Damn him.

If he was right about the elder royals being after her,

then it made sense that she should learn from the best. But...

"No way. Besides, you tend to piss me off."

"Which is exactly why you'll work twice as hard at punching me as you would with anyone else. If you're to have a chance—"

"I have no chance against an ancient vamp. None."

His hand moved toward the screen. "We'll see," he said, before ending the call.

Damn him! Even on video, he had to make a dramatic exit.

Scent

She'd taken the time to bathe after returning from London, and then changed into her running clothes, as she didn't own any gear, unlike basically anyone else in Oldcrest. Now there was no sense in delaying the inevitable. She left the dorms and headed north.

How many times had she watched this place from afar? Too many to count. But Chloe had never stepped anywhere near Night Hill until today.

The entire base of the hill was surrounded by electric fences, and it only had one opening: a gate barring the sinuous road leading up to the summit.

Once she reached the barrier, she frowned. There was no device, no camera, and the heavy black metal doors weren't moving. Maybe she should turn around. Go home now, while she still could.

But then Levi would—rightly—think that she'd chickened out like a coward. That wasn't an option.

She was chewing on her bottom lip when she caught movement in her peripheral vision; she lifted her gaze to see a familiar raven soaring in the sky, flying toward the hill. But instead of heading for her shoulder, the bird landed on a small building she hadn't even noticed.

To her right, a few hundred paces away, stood a small wooden cabin, its lights on so she could see someone moving inside.

Chloe cleared her throat as she reached it.

"Hello?"

Her voice sounded hoarse.

"Excuse me, I'm supposed to go up the hill."

Somehow.

She sighed when no one answered. Chloe glanced down at her phone in her hand. Levi hadn't called from a hidden number; she could just ring him and ask him to pick her up.

Like she was a helpless damsel in distress.

She lifted her fist and knocked at the door just as it swung open in front of the tallest person she'd ever seen.

He had a large head, flat at the top, and his face was contorted into a sullen expression. His eyes were moss-green, bright, and larger than her palm. The man was twice her size at least.

"I don't know you."

His voice was gruff.

"We haven't met before," she said reasonably, glad to hear that her voice was almost even. "My name is Chloe. Chloe Miller. I'm supposed to go on the hill—to see Levi."

The man narrowed his eyes. "I don't like lies."

Well, okay then.

"I'm not lying. We can call Levi and—"

"Why did you go and marry a Miller? Boring name. Not a bit of nobility in it."

Well, he was right about that.

"I didn't marry a Miller. That's my father's name."

His face wrinkled in an exaggerated frown, like the entire conversation confused him.

Then he turned back inside the small house.

"Chloe Miller, you say...Chloe Miller."

He returned with a long roll of paper and was now wearing a pair of gigantic glasses, thicker than the bottom of a wine bottle.

"Ah!" he exclaimed victoriously. "Chloe Miller. Currently blonde, brown eyes, five foot six." He looked up from his paper to take her in and nodded to himself. "Permitted on the hill since January. It appears all is in order, then. You may proceed."

She grinned at him. "Thank you. But you know my name, and it appears we're on unequal footing."

The man laughed good-humoredly. "Unequal footing is all you'll find on Night Hill. But you may have my name; I don't see why not. I'm Billevern. Bill. The last troll on Earth."

He said it quite proudly.

"Why the last?" Chloe couldn't help questioning.

The troll shrugged. "'Cause I have no interest in ladies. One doesn't reproduce when they prefer balls to lady bits."

Well, that made sense.

"Besides, I don't like children. And there are plenty of us in other worlds."

She had so many questions. Chloe had just opened her mouth, ready to spout them all out, when a familiar voice interrupted her.

"Chloe."

She turned and grimaced. Levi stood beside his flashy car and close to the now-open gate.

"I thought you might want a lift up the hill."

She sighed. "Until next time, then, Billevern."

She waved, and the troll waved back.

To her surprise, Levi circled the car to open the passenger door for her. He was old, but she wouldn't have thought of him as old-fashioned.

"Thanks."

She slid onto the leather seat; he'd shut the door and regained his place behind the wheel before she could tie her belt.

"Bill likes you."

She smiled. "He seemed nice enough."

"To you," Levi insisted. "He growls and bares his teeth at the rest of us. I think only a handful of people get a smile."

Chloe beamed. "That'd be because I'm polite. You're just annoying."

Levi's laugh was a low rumble. "Annoying that troll would be suicidal. He was trained alongside the slayers of old. His kind decide their likes and dislikes in a primal way. You either smell the right way, have pheromones he likes, or you don't. The human bullshit is just details."

She gave that statement a bit of thought. "So, wait, if I wear perfume, he might change his mind and dislike me?"

Levi shook his head as the car flew farther up the hill. She was glad he was driving her after all; if she'd had to hike all the way up, she might have arrived to training exhausted.

"Perfume just masks the surface. Most sups can still smell *you* underneath."

Interesting.

"What do I smell like?"

Levi's lips curved in a wicked smile. "Dessert."

She couldn't help herself: she laughed.

"Are we talking train macaroons or bread and butter pudding?"

He glanced at her, chuckling. "You want to know if you're appetizing?"

She shrugged. "If I'm food, I want to be out-of-this-world, orgasmic food, at least."

Levi shook his head, remaining silent.

"It's bread and butter pudding, isn't it?"

"Drop it, Chloe."

"I'm a common dessert. Woe is me!"

Levi swerved onto a driveway leading to an opulent red brick mansion that looked strangely modern, with floor-to-ceiling windows that took up most of the walls on the ground floor. The grounds weren't vast, but they'd been curved, cut, and trimmed into submission to look just as he willed them to. In front of the drive was a ridiculously large pool with an island in the center.

"That's a little..." She searched for a halfway polite word. "Much, don't you think?"

There were towers on either wing of the house. *Towers*.

"The estate has to be able to host gatherings of the gentry—thousands of vampires not easily impressed. And impressing them is a must."

She rolled her eyes. "You'd think so."

"Our kind have a short memory overall. Without subtle reminders, they soon forget who's in charge, and why."

"And the McMansion is a reminder?"

She undid her seatbelt; the next instant, her door was open and Levi was extending a hand to help her out.

"The armory, the paintings, the priceless sculptures by the most talented masters of this era certainly make a statement. And, well, we needed room to store all that shit."

Chuckling, she noticed that she wasn't nearly as annoyed with Levi as usual. There was something different about him tonight, although she wasn't sure what.

"Shall we?"

On Night Hill

The inside of the mansion didn't feel nearly as intimidating as its courtyard. Chloe wondered if Levi stuck to garden parties. The mansion actually felt a little homey, although no home of hers ever had original Greek sculptures.

She bent over the likeliness of a well-shaped naked man and smiled.

"No leaves?"

The Adonis's small prick was intact.

"No, the church has never had a reach here. Our art survived the sixteenth century nonsense, as well as any act of self-righteous human destruction either before or after."

Chloe had a feeling Levi didn't think much of her kind; he seldom mentioned humans without the word "nonsense" attached to it.

She was about to point that out when a delicate white cat with the brightest eyes she'd ever seen meowed, demanding attention. Chloe watched Levi's face soften.

"Don't believe her. I do, in fact, feed her."

The animal tiptoed down the grand wooden staircase, widening her beautiful eyes and rubbing against the banister.

Chloe couldn't resist. She headed right to the stairs and knelt before extending her hand to let the kitty sniff it.

"I wouldn't do—"

Too late. The warning had only been half-uttered when the animal's razor-sharp claws flashed, scratching the back of her palm deep enough to draw blood.

The cat licked her claw with a self-satisfied expression and returned to her rubbing.

Chloe laughed and got back to her feet. "My fault. I should have asked. Some cats are prickly. Animals usually like me, though."

Levi was silent. Chloe turned to him, and saw his gaze fixated on her hand.

Oh. Blood.

How easy it was to forget.

"Levi? Are you..." Going to eat me whole? "All right?"

He paused.

"Yes. I'm in control."

He didn't look in control. His eyes were fire, his jaw set. Chloe found herself missing the smirk that had irritated her so much in the past.

He was a predator after one thing, and like an idiot, she'd let herself forget that.

Levi took one step toward her, and then another. A third. He was right in front of her, close enough to touch. His nostrils flared.

Levi lowered his hand to hers and took it in his palm.

Then he brought it to his lips like a gentleman from an Austen novel. But instead of kissing her hand, he licked it, his tongue darting out once, his eyes remaining on hers.

"Lesson one. Your blood is your most powerful weapon. Use it well."

And on that note, he walked away, heading to a door left of the staircase.

Chloe learned to breathe again.

"Right. Can we elaborate on that lesson? It doesn't make much sense to those of us who aren't blood-sucking monsters."

"Get your ass over here, Miller."

The door led to a vast and mostly empty space with mats on the floor and training equipment scattered on the walls. The average Olympic gym had fewer toys.

Two vampires were sparring at one end of the room. Chloe watched with rapture as they moved fast and gracefully. She recognized them from the tower; the assistant and the woman had been rather amused by her outrage over being offered a coat.

Soon, the woman had the dark-skinned man on his back, and they stopped.

Chloe could have clapped. But the next moment, they were both gone.

"What the hell! Where did they go?"

At her side, Levi replied, "They're on patrol duty about now. This was just a quick training break."

Damn.

"You guys do take the whole training thing seriously."

"Yes. For one, our kind get relentless and it helps to focus our energy. But mostly because we have to fight for our lives every other century. Whoever wins is often whoever had the most training."

Which disqualified her.

"So how do I win?"

"You don't," he replied, point-blank.

"You give the best pep talk."

"Your goal isn't victory—not right now, not at your level. It's survival. You have friends. You have a guard. You have divine mojo in your bloodstream for the next few months."

She wondered how he knew about that. Chloe hadn't even told Mikar, feeling like it was huntsmen business she shouldn't share unless necessary. She was going to ask, but Levi continued, "The likelihood of any enemy having you to themselves for more than five minutes is practically nonexistent. The primary goal of your training is to teach you how to last five minutes against anyone."

She hated to admit it, but he made a lot of sense.

"All right. What does my blood have to do with that?"

"Most sups will smell it miles away. That makes it a liability, and also a weapon. You openly bleed anywhere within a mile, Mikar will follow the trail. But you may also use it against your opponent. They'll be focusing on trying to get to the blood—it may not even occur to them right away that they could simply rip out your throat. If your hand bleeds, they'll want your hand."

"So I can distract them," she said, catching on.

Levi inclined his head. "Precisely."

She nodded. "All right. Then what?"

"Then, you try to punch me."

She wasn't going to lie—at first, the prospect held some appeal, but she soon realized it had been a trap.

She drew her fist to the left, aiming for his shoulder, but he blocked, grabbed her wrist, and twisted it behind her back.

"Not bad. You need to be faster, and aim for the face —unless it's a feral, you want to stay as far as possible from the teeth. We'll get to that. Arms higher, use the other one to protect your face."

He let go of her wrist and took a step back.

"Again."

Two hours later, she really wanted to punch him. She was sweating, panting, and the man didn't even have the decency to look winded.

"Again!"

"If my arms fall off, it's your fault."

And her legs. And her lungs. Did she even have lungs?

She practiced the move he'd just shown her, a lower version of a skip-axe-kick, for the twelfth time, and the asshole casually stepped aside, effortlessly avoiding her.

Chloe dropped to the floor.

"Just give me five, okay?"

She was begging, and she wasn't even sorry. To her surprise, instead of admonishing her, Levi walked toward a fridge tucked in a corner of the room. He pulled out a bottle of water and handed it to her.

"Thank you."

"You're doing well, you know. Better than expected."

She rolled her eyes. "For a puny human?"

Levi shrugged. "For anyone. The art of violence is never easy, and particularly not at the start."

The art of violence. That certainly fit the way he moved.

"Would I have a chance, then?"

"Right now, no." At least he was no liar. "But give it time. All it takes is keeping your enemy out of range for one move, and then the next, and the one after that."

That sounded too simple.

"What were you saying earlier about the ferals? Those are the crazed-types we saw in London, right?"

A nod. "They're a different entity altogether. At this point, it's hard to even think of them as vampires."

Chloe frowned. "Mikar said they were sick vampires."

"In a way, yes, but there's no known cure. The ferals cannot stop themselves from gorging on blood. They bite and drain anything—vampire, human, shifter, demon, god, you name it. In most cases, they just kill their victims. But when they bite vampires, it's worse. They infect us."

Chloe grimaced. "So you could go all fangy?"

He snorted. "They'd have to get to me first." The lightheartedness disappeared fast. "They're too mindless to pose much of a threat to someone like me. And too slow. But their greatest strength is that they travel in packs. If you see one, there'll likely be a hundred on its heels. Against a vampire, you stand your ground and buy yourself time. Against a feral, don't hesitate. Run. Climb out of the way if you can. Hide. Use whatever artifice might fool a simple dog relying on its instincts."

She took in everything he shared, letting herself understand the implications. In the end, she only said one thing.

"Vampires are a lot faster than me."

He shrugged. "Your adrenaline will kick in. And muscle memory will help. More than you know. It's a wondrous thing. One day, you'll wake up and know all these moves. You'll know how to block, fight, lunge faster. You'll be able to anticipate your adversary's next move with just one hint."

Chloe wrinkled her nose. "I can't imagine getting to that point."

Especially against him. Levi grinned, extending his hand to help her up.

"Again."

A Blood Stone

CHAPTER

32

Her schedule got considerably more challenging; in addition to her usual classes, she took an hour of endurance with Professor Beaufort each morning, and learned to climb with Jack, who was a slave driver. Despite the wind, he insisted on practicing out of doors. The Institute training room had a perfectly good climbing wall, but it apparently wasn't good enough for Sir Sadist of Sade, who preferred to make her scrape her hands on the steep, calcareous walls of a hillside in the Wolvswoods.

On Thursday, she was told to head to the main gym.

The woman waiting for her was dark, sensual, beautiful, and mysterious. Her brown hair had red streaks in the sunlight, and while most of her features pointed to an Indian heritage, she had a dusting of freckles on her nose and green eyes that sparked with gold near the center.

Chloe didn't think she'd ever seen a more beautiful woman in her life.

"I'm Greer."

An unusual name Chloe had only heard once here. "As in Greer Vespian?"

"That's it."

She whistled, impressed.

She didn't know what she'd expected, exactly—someone a little more like Blair and Gwen, feminine, bubbly—but at a glance, Chloe would have pegged Greer as a huntsman. She had the look of a well-trained fighter and the analytical eyes of someone who knew how to put an adversary on their ass thirteen different ways.

"I've had some of your potions. You rock."

It was hard to tell under her ochre skin, but Chloe would have sworn the witch blushed.

"Thanks. I try. All right, so, I heard you've just taken up training."

Chloe winced. "Last weekend."

From her grimace, Greer seemed to understand her plight.

"Well, take it from someone who's been through this —sparring, running, obstacles; they'll make you strong. But without the basics, your body is just a list of limbs you don't really understand."

Chloe was ready for more torture. She was determined to never again feel as hopeless as she had in London, and if this was what it took, then she would go the distance.

"Right. What are we doing?"

Half an hour later, Chloe moaned in relief. Greer had made her lie on her back on a yoga mat and move her knees down to the floor on her right side while her head was turned the other way. Every single bone and muscle in her body thanked her for it. She was shown a few different twists and stretches to reconnect with her tense limbs, and when they were done training, Greer also handed her a bottle of gold liquid.

"That's to soothe your muscles. External use; just rub it after your bath every night like a moisturizer."

"What's in it?" Chloe asked, pocketing it.

Greer shrugged. "You know, essential oils, eucalyptus. Mostly magic, though. A mushroom that only grows at the very tip of a stiff cliff, flowers that must be picked on a blue moon, the raw heart of a..."

Chloe held her hands up in surrender. She didn't need to know whose heart she was ingesting. "Got it. No questions asked. If it helps, I'll use it."

The witch laughed. "Wise. Keep practicing, and I'll see you next week, same time?"

No way Chloe would miss that.

By the end of a long week, she was glaring every time her eyes fell on Night Hill, seeing it as the source of all her troubles. She was certain that if Levi had let Mikar, or basically anyone else, train her, every part of her flesh wouldn't feel like it had been beaten repetitively.

Except maybe Jack. She could be wrong, but she suspected that Jack's training plans might make Levi's seem like child's play.

To be fair, in just a week, she'd made considerable progress. She practiced the "block punch, grab, and twist arm" move Levi had used on her every day, moving against an invisible attacker, her hands only grabbing air —but she got faster and faster.

By Sunday, walking up to Night Hill, she was looking forward to showing her progress, although she wouldn't admit that to Levi.

He told her he'd pick her up at six at the bottom of

the hill, so she arrived at five-thirty, determined to speak to Bill again.

She knew something was wrong almost right away. Bill's cabin was dark and empty, its door wide open. Behind it and to the left, the gate heading up to Night Hill was open.

No, not open. Smashed. Destroyed.

Hearing and feeling movement behind her, she spun on her heels and breathed out in relief when Mikar appeared.

He lifted his arm, pointing east.

"On the hill. Now."

Not Night Hill. Coscnoc.

She opened her mouth. "No questions," he said. "You run, you hear me? Don't look behind you, run—through the woods, not on the trail. Don't trust *any* of your friends. One of them is behind this."

The next moment, he was running up Night Hill, leaving her side for the first time in three months.

Chloe stared at his back for a heartbeat. She'd never seen him so spooked, not even in London. What was he afraid of?

Don't trust any of your friends. One of them is behind this.

Behind what exactly? Breaking Night Hill's barrier? She didn't understand a thing.

But she did know one thing: Mikar had protected her since she'd entered Oldcrest. He had been a deterrent, at least, and maybe even a shield. And now, he was gone.

So, turning to face east, she ran.

At least she was good at running. The huntsmen hadn't dubbed her Cheetah for nothing.

Night Hill and Coscnoc were perhaps a mile apart,

separated by a muddy ravine. Any other day, she would have headed south, toward the Institute, and then north to Coscnoc, but the three-mile delay wasn't an option right now. She trekked through the mud, forcing herself to keep her gaze forward. Once she'd reached the base of the east hill, she glanced at her legs and grimaced.

"Sorry, pretty boots. I promise I'll clean and polish you."

If she survived whatever was happening.

Obeying Mikar's directions, Chloe remained away from the paths leading up to the summit, although running through the woods wasn't easy. When her lungs protested, she took a short break, using the opportunity to remove the mud at the sole of her boots on a tree trunk.

Then she leaned against it, closing her eyes.

What was going on?

Her eyes flew open. Someone was here. Again, surprise gave way to relief.

Levi.

"Oh my god, Levi. I don't know what's going on. Mikar...he told me to come here and then left. What's happening?"

Levi made no reply.

Something was wrong. He looked wrong.

No smirk, no smile. His eyes were hollow, void of emotion.

"Levi?"

Finally, he spoke.

"I didn't want it to be this way. Believe me."

What was he...

He advanced at the speed of light, making it clear

that until now, he had truly slowed himself down so she could see him, relax around him.

Don't trust any of your friends.

They weren't friends. Not truly. And Mikar wouldn't have warned her against *Levi*, his own master.

Chloe took one step back.

Too late. His hand was around her neck, keeping her in place. She didn't need to remember his lesson to know that she was screwed.

Yet she struggled, trying to break free. Of course she did; the dumbest animal would have done the same in her shoes. Levi's grasp tightened.

"Listen to me, Chloe. You're going to need this." He held up a chain with a strange metal pendant hanging from it, a dark stone at its center.

No, not a stone. A tiny flask filled with liquid.

Blood. It looked strange—wrong—but she knew, she just knew it was blood. Its faint scent. Coppery, heady.

"Do you understand me, Chloe?"

She shook her head as much as she could manage with his iron fist keeping her in place. She didn't understand a thing.

From the beginning, every single one of her instincts had been confused around him. Run away, run into his arms. Kiss him, plunge a knife into his chest. He'd infuriated her just by existing.

Still, her brain couldn't process everything. He was hurting her, and talking about a damn necklace.

There was a noise to her left. He let her turn her head.

She froze.

London had been nothing—*nothing*—compared to this.

She saw them running up the hill toward them. Hundreds of ferals, darkening the woods with their shadows.

But their greatest strength is that they travel in packs. If you see one, there'll likely be a hundred on its heels.

The next instant, the earth, sky, and wind were engulfing her. She felt sick to her stomach and taken by a tornado. Then the motion stopped as fast as it had started, and she found herself on solid ground.

Chloe blinked. They'd moved so very fast. They were hundreds of feet up, still on Coscnoc.

"There's no escaping the hill now," he said, hand still on her throat, another one around her waist.

His grip was the only thing keeping her upright.

"We're surrounded. And lower down the hill, the masters who unleashed the ferals on us are waiting for us. If I tried to get you out of here, I'd fail. They'd fight, and the moment you're out of my reach, they would destroy you. Rip out your heart. Behead you. Nod if you heard me."

So many words, all meaning one thing.

She was going to be killed. Someone would manage to get to her. There was no hope of getting out of this.

She sniffed. "Why? Why do they—"

Her voice broke. Did it matter why?

"We don't have time, Chloe. Not now. Remember everything I've said. Focus on it. Can you do that?"

It didn't sound like he was trying to hurt her after all. She swallowed with difficulty and nodded.

"Good girl. I'll see you on the other side."

She wanted to ask what he meant.

But he'd snapped her neck, and she was already dead.

Control

T *hree months ago*

"*YOU'VE TAMED A MAGNIFICENT BEAST, LEVIATHAN,*" THE goddess had said, so long ago. "*And a clever one. Do as you please but heed my warning. If the creature inside you stirs, you would do well to listen to it.*"

Levi had been a wild thing in his youth. Passionate about right and wrong, ready to right wrongs and fight for those who couldn't stand up for themselves.

Then, he'd grown up. Realized that fangs, claws, and the monsters of the deep sea couldn't solve a thing. And he'd used his skills another way. His mind was superior to most immortals, and he bent it toward finding cures to the most devastating illnesses, inventing devices that saved lives. He was a scientist, and proud of it.

Fifteen hundred years had passed since Ariadne had

said those words to him, and not once had he needed to listen to her advice.

Until that night.

The beast was rushing to the surface, desperate to be freed.

Levi let it run. All night and most of the morning, as fast as he could, without rest. Run, run, run. He didn't understand it; he just knew he had to get there.

His steps took him to a familiar gray city awakening in the rain.

London.

His clothes were torn and his shoes had holes. Levi headed to the home he kept in Kensington to change as fast as possible, and he followed the call pulling him forward, like a passenger along for the drive.

That's when he saw her for the first time, and he knew right then.

She would have died if he hadn't made it.

He knew her name. He'd seen a picture of her before, attached to a file. A prospective student at the Institute.

Chloe.

When she'd just been a name and a picture, he hadn't understood. Now that she was in front of him, now that he smelled and felt her, he got it.

She was one of them. A fledgling well in transition.

And something more.

Someone had gone to great lengths to get to her without dirtying their hands. Why? It made no sense. Born vampires were rare but relatively inconsequential. Their kind saw them as something precious, because only one or so was born per century, but they had little power until they gained experience and skills after turning.

Why was a noble trying to destroy *her*?

It didn't matter. Levi just knew that she was his.

His responsibility.

His...

Shit.

Part of him wanted to walk up to her and slit her throat now. Get it over with. To complete the transition, they had to let their mortal selves perish. A traumatic experience for anyone, even those who'd been prepared their entire life. But one look in her big blue eyes and he knew she was ignorant, innocent, in need of care and time.

He'd give her both. As long as he could.

☙❧

Now, she was in his arms, lifeless, pale, and cold. Levi wished he'd explained things, told her on that very first day that it was always going to come to this. She would have to die.

She'd been too cheerful and insouciant, and he, cowardly. She wouldn't forgive him for making this so brutal.

Chloe stirred, exhaling deeply, swallowing as much air as her lungs could carry.

Her hands were trembling, her eyes filled with tears. But she moved fast. Faster than him.

He wasn't surprised when she managed to flip him over and squeeze his throat.

From the start, the creature inside her had revolted

against him, against his authority, because she was more dominant than him. Stronger than him.

It hadn't quite made sense. He'd had theories, but the truth only became certain when he'd received an unexpected visit.

❧

Two months ago

A SLAYER WAS AT HIS DOOR, ESCORTING A CREATURE who shouldn't have existed.

Dark hair. Eyes so blue they lit up the room more than his lamp.

"My name is Tom Miller," he'd said. "I'm Chloe's older brother."

That much was obvious, but he was also something else.

A born vampire, fully turned only recently. And with an aura as powerful as Levi's.

"Miller," Levi repeated with a snort. "I find that unlikely."

The guy had inclined his head. "Well, that's the name I was born with. But, all right. If you prefer, I'm Thomas Eirikrson."

His wildest suspicion, perhaps his greatest fear.

There was a new Eirikrson. Two of them, actually.

And it was his fault.

Levi had spared their ancestor during the purge, so many eons ago, pulling a little boy out of the way. And through him, their line had endured.

What now?

The Eirikrsons were monsters. Always had been to the core. They'd taken to lording over the rest of their race, assassinating those who stepped out of line, but that was just an excuse to satisfy their bloodthirst. Levi hadn't partaken in the purge, but he hadn't disapproved either.

The obvious answer was to kill the boy, and the girl too.

But he couldn't.

Because for better or worse, Chloe Eirikrson was his mate, and he couldn't bring himself to destroy her. He wasn't suicidal. Killing his own mate would be just that: damning himself.

"I'm surprised I haven't heard that the House of Eirikr has risen again."

"Are you?" Tom had asked. "Surprised."

Not really.

Tom had obviously stayed in the shadows to protect his sister while she was mortal.

"Why do you come to me now?"

"Because you're smart," his slayer companion said. "Smart enough to at least suspect what she was—and yet, you haven't attempted to hurt her. And because, if I'm not mistaken, you're the one who saved their house in the first place."

He'd never liked Viola much. Now he knew why. She was too clever by half.

"What do you want of me?"

The boy extended his hand. He was holding a necklace.

"My blood. She'll need it to change. We had the pendant spelled; it'll last a year or so."

"Why not give it to her, then?" Levi asked.

He expected the answer. "She doesn't know a thing. I didn't either, until a few years ago. And we're trying to keep it that way, because everyone could be a spy, an enemy. I'll try to be around when she needs it, but Viola and I aren't always in the country. In case something happens to me, at least there's a safeguard."

"Do you expect something to happen to you?" Levi had questioned, relatively indifferent one way or another.

Viola was the one who answered.

"I'm sure you've noticed the movements around the other families, Leviathan. The Stormhales have gone quiet. The Beauforts have all returned to France, except for that stubborn teacher in your school. They're all plotting, and it started after the results of Tom's blood tests hit the web. They know there are Eirikrsons left. And they know that if they actually manage to annihilate the line for good this time, Skyhall, its treasures, and its power will be fair game. Can you imagine? Since the Eirikrsons, there's been no real leader for our kind. But if they can absorb the essence of that line's power..."

He could imagine, and damn her, but Viola was right.

That sort of power shouldn't be in anyone's hand.

The problem was that right now, it was at the tip of Tom's finger.

"You're the head of the Eirikrsons," Levi told the boy. "You could make us kneel and dance to your tune, like a child playing with chess pieces."

The boy laughed.

"If you think I'm in charge, you clearly don't know my sister."

LEVI HAD DOUBTED TOM AT THE TIME. CHLOE WAS too nice. Too charming. Everyone loved her. She definitely hadn't seemed like his idea of a sovereign.

Then he'd understood.

The creature inside him was a straightforward beast, always up for bloodsport, attacking head-on.

Hers was a spider, weaving webs around people's hearts and playing them to her tune, consciously or not.

Right now, Levi could feel them. Dozens of huntsmen, Mikar, Cat, Bill, half a dozen witches, all fighting their way through legions of ferals to get to her.

He'd feared that her family would try to rule vampirekind by fear. What she was doing was a thousand times worse.

She would rule all, with nothing but a pretty smile.

The evening sky darkened under a cloud of ravens flying atop the hill, gathering around their master.

She remained still, grasping his throat.

"Why am I alive?" she finally said, her throat dry, obviously sore.

"Because you're a born vampire. Your blood. Drink it now. Without it, you..."

He didn't finish the sentence, eyes widening in horror.

She'd pulled the necklace up to eye level. And at the center, the stone was broken.

One Course

L evi froze beneath her, horror echoing in his every feature, eyes widened in shock, mouth hanging. It was bad. She could tell it was bad, even in her fuzzy, hazy mind. Levi had never once looked like this. In a fraction of a second, her mind ran through every time she'd seen him. Nope. No horror anywhere.

Her eyes returned to the broken stone. Red blood. A faint scent that wasn't any less familiar. She would have recognized it anywhere.

This was the scent of Sunday pancakes and bad jokes. Home.

"Tom."

She didn't think she'd said the name in years. Not since then. After her father's arrest, the world had opened up under her feet, and she'd turned every which way in an attempt to find her anchor, but he'd been gone. He'd abandoned her.

All the hurt she'd long buried rushed to the surface, fueling a rising rage she didn't know where to direct.

There was a man on his back beneath her knees. Him. She could destroy him. She'd feel better after, right?

No. Not him.

The thing inside her had had a presence, thoughts that never quite matched her own, until this day. Now, they were in agreement, and it had a voice. Her voice, whispering words of darkness at the back of her mind.

"Chloe, *focus*," Levi said. "You've unlocked a hundred percent of your brain functions, and it can be confusing, but you just need to concentrate on what's important. The ferals. Getting out of here. You understand?"

Ferals. Yes, that rang a bell.

She could definitely destroy them. She grinned.

"*Chloe...*"

She was already on her feet, running downhill. They were close. Now that her attention was on them, she could hear them, feel them.

A piercing cry resounded, and her eyes turned skyward. Ravens. All of the ravens in the message box, and more. They were following her.

She liked it. She liked them. She wanted to be with them.

Her heart became lighter, and she almost felt herself float, when a hand grabbed hold of her wrist and pushed her hard against a tree.

"Listen to me, child," Levi roared.

Chloe bared her teeth. "I'm no child."

"Then stop acting like one. Carry on and you will *die*. For good. Not even because of the ferals, not because of the gentry waiting for you at the bottom of this hill. Because without the blood of your clan, you're nothing but a corpse on borrowed time."

It was hard, so very hard, to truly take in anything—

there was so much to look at and listen to. Her memories. The sound of the wildlife running in every direction, fleeing from the monsters. The ferals. A fight. The moon rising in the distance. After darkness fell, the world had been shadows to her until now. Now she saw through the fog, and it was beautiful.

She didn't want it to end. Not now. The thing inside her didn't either. It forced her to pay attention. Not just to Levi's words—to herself.

Her limbs had felt like they could soar, like she was stronger than anything—anyone.

Now she noticed the decline. The fatigue. How very dry her throat was, like sanding paper. Her hands, so strong a minute ago, were trembling.

"What's happening to me?"

"You're mid-transition, and you need Tom's blood. You have a night, at most, if you save your energy. Your stunt trying to sync with your raven familiars already cost you."

Shit.

She had no clue what he meant about syncing, but she certainly felt drained. Enfeebled, unexplainably.

"Next time, how about you warn a girl?" she retorted, without much heat, mainly because she didn't have the energy to summon up the requisite amount of ire.

"How about we concentrate on keeping you alive? You can tell me everything I did wrong if you're breathing by dawn."

Dawn seemed so far when night had only just claimed dominion over the hill.

Their heads snapped downhill as shadows approached.

The ferals.

Levi let go of her and turned to face them.

"You remember what I said last week?"

Yes. No. Maybe.

Thankfully, he spelled it out for her. "Run."

Oh. That.

She hesitated.

"What about you?"

He glanced over his shoulder. "Don't insult me. I'll wipe the floor with that lot without breaking a sweat."

She knew he could take care of himself, but she could only concentrate on what he'd once said, how one feral bite was enough to turn any vampire into a mindless creature. What if they took him by surprise? Someone had to watch his back.

She stood her ground as the first line closed in on Levi.

Until now, she'd always seen a blur of unclear movements—one moment Levi was standing to her right, then to her left, and she couldn't detect the transition. Now, she saw everything, each of his graceful, precise moves. A leap to the first feral, his knee colliding with the side of its jaw, then using his neck to pivot mid-air, his boot kicking down three of them in one blow. The man was a machine.

A machine fighting one against a hundred.

She rushed forward just as someone leaped in the air, landing right in front of her on a crouch. Jack was still wearing a damn suit, not one hair out of place.

He watched her, his jaw tight.

Right. Her friend disliked vampires. She'd forgotten.

Chloe wondered how obvious her change had been. Did she have fangs? Was there something different in her eyes? Did he hate her now?

Jack pulled knives from inside his jacket and threw them close to Levi. The vampire didn't even flinch as they lodged inside the skulls of ferals either side of him.

"Let's see if you can live up to your name, Cheetah. Get out of here."

Maybe he didn't hate her after all. She grinned before saluting and turning her heels away from the fight.

Leaving them was harder than anything she'd ever done, but they were both seasoned fighters, and she knew she'd only be in the way if she stayed. A liability. They might get hurt trying to help her, too.

So, she ran—at first, anyway. It soon became much harder than she'd anticipated. Chloe wasn't much of a cheetah right now—her sides hurt, and she was out of breath and sweating like a pig.

"I smelled something this way."

She froze. She'd never heard that voice. Chloe hadn't asked, but she doubted ferals talked; not in an enunciated way, in any case.

There was a very high probability that some of the gentries were after her. Old, well-trained vampires. At the best of times, she wouldn't have had much of a chance. Right now, feeling so diminished? There was zero hope. Levi had told her to buy herself time until help came, but right now, he, and all her friends, had their hands full.

She needed to hide. But where? They could smell her, hear her. She looked around, panicked.

Then her eyes fell north. She couldn't see it from here, but she knew the way. The path.

In a cave, protected by so many spells your head will spin just going anywhere near it.

He was insane.

Monster.

So many words. So many warnings. All cautioning her to go nowhere near the cave on the hill.

But did she have a choice?

A Voice in the Darkness

CHAPTER
35

By the time she'd reached the crossroads, Chloe moved like a puppet with broken strings. She needed to stop. She needed air. Rest. Sleep. But she put one foot after the other, again and again. Past the black tape, through the sinuous, uneven path.

It was a miracle no one had caught her yet. The moment they did, she was gone.

She glanced behind her.

Was it a miracle? She could feel something in the air. A thin, immaterial veil between her and the rest of the world. Magic.

It was faint, but she could sense magic around her.

She remembered. The things in her blood. Nanocytes, Jake's father had said. They were masking her presence, somehow. Hiding her smell, maybe even her noise. They wouldn't help if someone stumbled upon her, but at least no one could hunt her down using their senses.

She needed to send the huntsman a thank-you card. After dawn. If there was a dawn.

The trail continued forever. As she walked further, the foliage became denser, taking over the long-untrodden path.

Was she far enough from the main path? Mikar had said there were spells keeping intruders out, but she hadn't felt anything yet. Would the talks and legends be enough to prevent those hunting her from following her here?

Chloe stilled her resolve. She doubted the ferals remembered the tales, if they'd ever known them. To escape them, she had to find the wards and pass them.

She kept walking, groaning, panting.

Too many had fought—were still fighting—so that she may live. She wouldn't insult them by giving up just because it was hard.

One more step. And another one. A third...

She felt it when she hit the barrier. Ahead of her was an old staircase carved into the stone so long ago it almost looked like a natural slide. It wasn't. Around the staircase was an open doorway leading down into the darkness. Inscriptions that Chloe couldn't read were written all around them. But between the door and her was an immaterial, shimmery wall that made everything seem darker on the other side.

She'd learned enough of magic to be wary. This could mean death. The person who dared pass might disintegrate on contact, or worse.

She looked behind her to the empty path. Her ears, so much more efficient now, could still heard the vampires on the main path. Arguing. They didn't want to follow her, knowing what awaited.

"Can you imagine going to the queen and telling her we didn't follow that trail because we were scared of a monster long turned to stone—if he ever existed? We have to go."

"After you, then."

"I know. Let's call the beasts. If the ferals make it..."

She looked back at the wall.

"Whatever luck I've had until now, please, please don't let me down."

She'd never said anything that resembled a prayer as much as this.

Chloe stepped forward.

Nothing. The barrier did...nothing.

She'd gone beyond.

Chloe would have laughed, if she had the energy. And if she hadn't realized something else: the wall hadn't been erected to prevent things from going *in*.

She walked forward, calling down the stairs.

"Hello?"

No answer, just the whisper of the wind.

She sighed in relief.

Well, she couldn't very well stay here, in any case; anyone walking the path would see her.

She started to walk down the steps, careful not to trip on the slippery rock.

Tired as she was, the descent seemed to take forever, but she finally arrived in an empty, dark, and damp chamber carved in the belly of the mountain.

She looked around and, finding nothing, slumped on the floor, throwing her head back.

Finally. Rest. Now if she could only close her eyes...

"Don't."

Chloe froze. There was nothing around. Her vision was clear, even in the darkness, and she didn't see anyone at all.

"Don't close your eyes, little daughter. You're already fading from this world."

She got to her feet with great effort and walked to the center of the room, looking around.

"Where are you?"

"Not far."

"Why can't I see you?"

"You will not wish to gaze upon me. You're frightened enough."

She huffed. "Right. Because hearing voices without seeing their source isn't frightening at all."

A second passed as Chloe once more wished she'd held her tongue.

The thing in front of her was terrifying. A frail, graying corpse with eyes too bright and no substance at all, like a dried-up mummy.

She gasped.

"Stay here for a few thousand years and we'll see how pretty you are then."

His voice was so light, teasing. And even in his state, she could tell he was smiling. It was a horrifying smile, but a smile nonetheless.

"You're Eirikr," she said.

The mummyish corpse inclined his head. Long silver-white strands of hair were still attached to his skull.

"You look terrible."

"I see you inherited my tact and kindness."

Inherited. He said it like...

But she knew that. Somehow, she'd suspected she was linked to him so long ago. When she'd stood at the end of the path leading to his cave. When she'd been told there were seven families, and Blair had refused to talk of the last. She'd been incredibly frustrated. Tell me, she'd wanted to scream.

Tell me about my family.

"What's your name, little daughter?"

She cleared her throat.

"Chloe. Chloe Miller..."

"Chloe Eirikrson," he corrected. "That's what they'll all call you, whispering behind your back like it's a curse. You may as well claim the benefits."

She didn't understand what he meant.

"Because you went crazy?"

The corpse seemed to smile again. "Our kind have unlimited power here. We outnumber all those who could tame us on Earth. And we outpower everyone else. For long—too long—vampires lived as gods, taming humanity under their heels. I was focused on my own missions, ignoring their barbarism. Then, I looked at the world and decided to change it. I forced them all back into the shadows. Because I am the monster they fear, and fear means respect."

Even now, so frail and all but exsanguinated, he held an air of power that made her believe every word.

"Then they locked you up."

He inclined his head. "But my heirs continued my work. And when they, too, were betrayed, the huntsmen I'd armed had grown powerful enough to pose a real threat. So, our pestilential species didn't slaughter their way through countless mortals with impunity, as they used to."

There were always three sides to the story. She'd heard and doubted the one her friends knew. Now she heard and doubted his. She suspected the truth was somewhere in the middle.

Not that it mattered. Nothing mattered anymore. She felt it. She had moments. Minutes, if that.

Chloe knew the blood of an ancestor was the answer, but she didn't ask for his. Even she could see that he had none to give. No more than a drop coursed through his veins.

"Don't despair yet, little daughter. Help is on the way."

She blinked, cheering up.

"Tom?"

The creature's eyes flashed. "Not quite."

Then, he was gone. A burst of wind heading up the stairs.

With her new immortal eyes, she'd been able to detect Levi's movements, but she couldn't see his. She doubted anyone could. Frail, powerless, decaying.

Eirikr was none of these things.

Monsters

She heard the screams. The heart-wrenching yells. The pleas.

"Spare me, I beg you. I'll serve you!"

And the horrifying crushing sound of bone breaking.

Then the smell. Blood. So much blood flowing.

Chloe heard suctioning, gulping, and then an appreciative moan.

She was going to be sick.

After killing and draining she didn't know how many of her pursuants, Eirikr walked back down to the cave.

Chloe couldn't believe her eyes.

The dry corpse was gone, replaced by a man so handsome he put Levi to shame. The portrait in the huntsmen's quarters in London hadn't done him justice. Lean, with a muscular, well-built frame. The rag on his hips looked like the remnants of a kilt that once had some color. There was mud and blood on his golden skin, which she felt looked very natural and appropriate on a predator.

Eirikr looked like her brother Tom. He even had the

same hair as the rest of her family—dark at the roots and then unnaturally light an inch later.

No one would have doubted that they were family. A family of crazy, beautiful creatures that didn't belong to this world.

"Better, don't you think?"

She had no words.

Eirikr brought his wrist to his lip and bit down, drawing blood. At least she thought it was blood. But it was black—dark as night.

She looked up to his eyes as he reached out, close to her mouth.

Nothing had ever smelled as appetizing. Not even candy. She wanted that blood like she wanted her next breath.

But there was something else she wanted more.

"I can't..."

She closed her eyes, the smell of his blood making her feel dizzy, mindless. Uncontrollable.

"I can't be a monster," she finished.

She couldn't become her father. Or end up locked in a cage like Eirikr because everyone was afraid of her. Better for her to leave this world now, when everyone could recall her with fondness, than to linger as a thing from their nightmares.

Eirikr tilted his head.

"Then who will? I have no way out of here, and your brother is no leader. Who will stand when the world needs justice?"

She shook her head, too weak to argue. Plenty of other people were more suited to the task. Tris, Jack, and the rest of the huntsmen. Levi, who could move like lightning and command the likes of Cat and Mikar. Anyone.

"Chloe, you were born to lead our house into the light. Because you have compassion, heart, and strength. Without you, our kind will rise again. There will be another Age of Blood, and none to stop our rule. The six clans will systematically destroy all threats—the witches, the huntsmen, anyone with a good heart, while they're scattered. You will unite them. You can rule all."

She snorted. That certainly was another level of flattery.

"Right."

Just one word, but it dripped with the perfect amount of sarcasm.

This time, Eirikr's smile was devastatingly beautiful.

"Prove me wrong, then. Unless you're a coward. Which would be unseemly. My house has never fathered any spineless wenches."

Anger. He was trying to provoke her, and it was working, awakening her mind a bit.

She was no coward. She was just...

Tired. So very tired.

"As we debate, one of your friends is dying. There is no stopping it, but how many will follow? Another one has been bitten by a feral. Will you wallow in self-pity at my feet when the blood in our veins is the only cure?"

Her eyes widened.

"Who...where—" As difficult as it was, she closed her mouth to swallow some saliva before forcing out a complete sentence. "I thought there was no cure?"

Levi had said a feral's bite was contagious and impossible to reverse.

"There wasn't. Not with me stuck in here and your mortal blood still running through your veins."

She was confused, and to her relief, Eirikr didn't wait for her to ask questions before explaining, "I do not drink human blood. From the very beginning, my everything recoiled against it, and for a time, I drained whatever game I could hunt in the woods—bears, deer, even rats. But as Ariadne's sickness spread through the lands, I found another food source." His lip curled over his teeth. He had two elongated canines on each side.

Then she understood. He drank vampire blood, not human blood.

And he wasn't crazy.

"My house has evolved to survive on vampire blood without giving in to the frenzy that renders the ferals mindless. Those two thousand years of evolution course through your veins. A few drops of your blood would be enough to reverse the process."

Then Eirikr extended his arm again. His dark blood still marred his skin, but the wound he'd inflicted on himself had long been healed.

"Drink, little daughter. Drink and rise. For their sake, if not yours."

She wrapped her fingers around his forearm. Her eyes focused on the veins. The blood moved faster at each of Eirikr's slow heartbeats.

She felt a strange numbing pain around her gums and tasted iron in her mouth. Her blood. Sweeter than she remembered. Unfamiliar.

Chloe opened her mouth wide to accommodate her new fangs, then closed it around her ancestor's wrist, trying to aim for the veins.

And then she drank.

And drank, and drank again.

She'd never been one to get drunk, because no cocktail had ever been so succulent, heady, addictive. She moaned in delight, holding on to Eirikr's arm with her second hand.

He laughed.

"Try not to drain me, will you? It has been long since I've enjoyed the benefits of having a decent amount of blood in my system."

Oh. Right.

Chloe let go of his arm. Right. She was drinking from a person, not a martini glass with a little umbrella.

"Sorry?"

He shrugged off her apology.

"How do you feel?"

She paused, having failed to notice any difference, but now that he pointed it out, she was...good.

Great.

The very notion of having been exhausted, spent, and ready to give up moments ago confused her.

She got to her feet, wondering why she'd been on her knees at all.

How did she feel?

Restless. Unfocused. Chaotic.

But above all...

"Angry," she replied.

Eirikr grinned.

"Good."

Newborn

Whoever was behind the attack had been smart, Levi had to give them that. Sending their feral dogs first had ensured that the huntsmen and knights alike were occupied, and then their foot soldiers had been scattered throughout the unmanned territory.

Levi and the huntsman at his back made short work of the group they'd encountered before sending Chloe on her way, then headed downhill to aid the others.

It wasn't pretty.

Levi hadn't dealt with huntsmen for an age, but he had to admit that they could certainly be useful. Not all of them were Jack Hunter, however. They were losing ground.

Another hundred ferals had surrounded three of them, two young men and a woman who was quite gifted with her many knives. Her, he knew of. They weren't acquainted, but there was only a handful of born vampires at any given time, and Levi made a point to remember their faces. Tris. Adrian's daughter. He positioned himself as her six, guarding her back as they fought through that lot.

Once they were dealt with, Levi said, "I hear three other groups—two south, one east. Let's split."

Jack went south with the boys while Tris headed east with him.

She froze as they arrived, screaming, "Bash!"

The warning came too late. A feral behind the huntsman plunged its eight sharp fangs into his shoulder. From where he stood, Levi could smell the blood; it had broken the skin, which meant the man was already lost.

Most would have fallen and screamed in agony, but Bash was strong. Not only did he remain on his feet, he also kept fighting, swinging his ax at any threat around him.

Levi held Tris's arm as she rushed toward her friend. She glared at him, but he just shook his head.

"There's nothing to do now. If you get close…"

"Touch me again, you lose that arm," the woman growled.

She would make a devastating immortal when she changed.

If she didn't turn feral first.

"If you want to help your friend, let's clear the beasts," Levi told her.

She seemed to agree.

The woman launched herself at them with a battle cry. Levi was no less brutal. He hated losing lives, even those he didn't know. Hence why he remained on his hill, in his tower, behind a red door. Out here, people died, or worse.

One head ripped off. A knife through a heart. A kick

so hard it cracked a skull. One after the next, they fell, until there was silence.

Levi turned to the huntsman. Bash.

He'd given up standing and was now panting hard.

His friends were approaching.

"Stay away," Bash said before Levi could caution them against getting too close. "I feel..."

Levi knew how he felt.

He took one step. Right away, four weapons were unsheathed as the huntsmen focused on him.

They knew what his kind did to those who were turned when they wished to be kind. Give them a quick death.

He held his hands up in the air.

"I won't hurt him. I can make him sleep, however. He won't feel pain through the change."

"Is that a euphemism for death? Try, bloodsucker. We'll see who'll go to sleep."

They certainly didn't lack guts.

"Children, quiet. I don't intend to dispense with a perfectly good test subject."

Cold, but true. And hopefully, it would get the point across.

"I keep ferals for observation while I work on a cure. If we take him to my lab..."

"Is there one?" Tris asked, her voice breaking. "A cure?"

Levi shook his head. "Not yet."

He wished he could give a different answer, but he wasn't one to lie.

"I want to go. In the lab. I want to go," Bash said, proving to be the wisest of the five.

Levi walked forward again, pulling one of Alexius's

potions out of his jacket, glad he'd taken to keeping the sleeping draught with him.

"Drink this."

The huntsman obeyed, and faded almost right away.

Now that this immediate potential threat was dealt with, Levi listened to his surroundings. No more large groups, but he heard and felt plenty of intruders.

He pulled keys out of his pocket and threw them at the fledgling.

"You should be able to slip out now, if you take the ravine west. Head to Night Hill, last house before Skyhall. When you go in, there's a study to the right. You'll find suitable restraints in the chest of drawers. Do not leave him without chains."

The girl nodded. He hoped she obeyed. Students turning feral en masse was the last thing he needed right now.

One huntsman carried each of Bash's arms, a third walked in front, and the fourth closed the circle as they walked away. Levi started to hunt.

Clearing ferals wasn't fun. It equated to having a rat infestation. But hunting down vampires in full control of their senses was another matter altogether. Levi knew they heard him coming, felt the air cool as he closed in on them. He watched true fear in their eyes before bringing them to their knees.

Killing a vampire wasn't easy. He couldn't just slit throats; that sort of wound could heal. He had to cut through the spine, rip out the heart. Fire or water could have done the job, but as he had none at hand, he had his work cut out.

At first, Levi ripped his way through skeletons,

ignoring the blood on his hands, but as the number of enemies thinned, he changed tactics.

Finding a group of three, he made quick work of the first two, and then wrapped his bloody hand around the third's throat before pulling him off his feet and holding him high.

"Who sent you?"

The first four vampires he questioned could not answer. They choked on any reply, not only because he was strangling them. Something prevented them from speaking.

"True to the blood!" is what most would say.

Just those four words.

They were bound by magic, that much was obvious. Dammit. He stopped attempting to spare anyone, instead focusing on clearing his territory and, more importantly, finding Chloe.

He couldn't sense her location, not even through the faint bond that had always existed between them.

As if she was fading. Losing energy. And no wonder.

He couldn't focus on that now. First, he had to kill the enemy to protect Oldcrest, his home, the hundreds of students here. Then, he'd find her.

She was alive. He had to believe that. He'd find her and then hunt Tom down to get more blood for her. Or demand it from Ariadne herself if that's what it took.

He had to...

Levi stopped in his tracks midway through striking a curly-haired blond vampire near Eirikr's cave.

Fire.

As sure as there was water in his soul, the woman in front of him was all raging blue fire.

There was nothing sweet about her. Nothing beautiful. She was too terrifying to be called that. Bewitching, fascinating, and irresistible would work, though.

Chloe moved like a shadow, kicking the blond's head and pushing the heel of her muddy boot into his chest.

"Who sent you?"

The man looked frantic as he struggled to break free. She pushed more of her weight forward, leaning in.

"Who?"

Her voice was so very beautiful, melodious, like honeysuckle.

"We serve the queen," he replied weakly. "She said there was an imposter. Someone who wanted to take everything she's worked for these past hundred years. We were told it'd be a human girl with tricks."

The vampire looked ashamed now.

"What queen?" Levi asked.

Many bore the title. A hundred queens ruled around the world.

"The queen of all vampires," he replied.

Levi frowned. No such thing existed.

"She will have us give in to our true nature, hunt and celebrate darkness, once all who oppose her are gone. The queen will bring back the golden age, as it was foretold."

That explained it. Fanatics.

"A name," Chloe demanded.

The vampire shook his head. "There is none. She is the queen."

Well, that was certainly convenient.

Pointy Things

The terrified vampire had nothing more to tell them. Chloe drew her leg back and tilted her head.

"On your way, then."

The curly-haired blond vampire was confused. He no doubt expected to end up like the various pieces of bodies littering the ground. And that would have been his fate had he not talked.

"If we kill everyone, who will be left to tell that queen of yours that we are not to be trifled with?"

Levi didn't contradict her.

The vampire started to walk away, glancing back as if to ensure they weren't changing their minds and preparing to attack from behind. Once he'd put a fair distance between them, he started to run.

Levi was looking at her strangely, half-careful, half-admiring. Chloe decided she liked it.

"I heard someone was wounded. Bitten," she corrected.

He nodded. "Bash. How..."

How had she heard, how was she alive and healed—whatever his question, there was one answer.

"Eirikr."

She was almost amused by his puzzlement, but there were more important matters. "Where's Bash?"

"My place. Chloe, there's..."

Without waiting to hear any more, she began running downhill as fast as she could.

Turned out, that was a lot faster than she would have imagined. She retreated the way she'd come, through the muddy ravine, avoiding all threats in her haste. Eirikr had told her she could save Bash, and she believed him, but if he attacked one of the others and they had to destroy him before she got there, it would be too late.

She was in front of the ridiculously large mansion in seconds, having crossed four miles down and then uphill again in under a minute.

This vampire thing was turning out to be more fun than she thought. Bonus, she'd yet to feel like skinning anyone alive.

She'd only just crossed the door when three huntsmen rushed out, weapons at hand.

They stilled before her.

"Jesus H. Christ, Cheetah."

Yeah, they had questions. So did she.

All of them could wait.

"Where's Bash?"

Tris gestured to the door on the right.

"It's best if you keep your distance. Blair and Gwen are trying to slow down the change. He's fighting them, although he's just taken a sleeping draught that should have knocked him out. He's restrained, but..."

She was already at the door.

Bash was lying on a ruby-red velvet sofa, his arms crossed on his chest, his upper body in chains. His eyes were shut, yet he writhed and groaned, his teeth biting the air.

Blair was holding on to his forehead, chanting. Her kindness had overwritten her caution. Gwen was no better, holding his torso so he couldn't move too much.

"Chloe! Stay away, he's extremely dangerous."

Her change had been obvious to Levi and the huntsmen, but the witches didn't seem to have caught on yet. Probably because their attention was focused on Bash.

"It's fine. I have a cure."

She could feel everyone freeze as she held out her wrist.

Mid-move, she realized that baring her teeth right now wasn't the smartest move.

"Anyone have a knife?"

When Tris was in the room, the answer to that question was always yes. She threw one of her knives and Chloe caught it with no effort. She sliced her wrist, wincing at the sharp pain, and held it up right in front of Bash's open mouth.

She had to admit, she gasped along with everyone else.

She hadn't expected this.

Earlier today, her blood had been just as red as the sofa. She'd never thought that part of her had changed, but if it had, she expected it to become black like Eirikr's. To her relief, it wasn't.

The blood was amethyst. A bright shade of darker purple, as unnatural as it was fascinating. Her scattered brain couldn't help admiring it. Then, under her arm, Bash sighed deeply and settled on the sofa. Smiling, she pulled her hand back and concentrated on her friend. His chest was rising and falling. He'd be fine.

Right?

But deep down, she knew he wouldn't be. Not truly. She'd cured him from the feral bite, yes, but Bash had been killed and, while he lingered in darkness, given vampire blood.

When he woke, he wouldn't be the same.

This was better than the alternative, though.

She got up and turned to the silent room.

"All right, so this calls for hot chocolate. Where's the kitchen?"

THEY DIDN'T FIND THE KITCHEN, ALTHOUGH THEY stumbled upon various fascinating rooms—two torture chambers, a lab Frankenstein would have been proud of, and a hall full of weapons that Bat whistled upon seeing.

"Dude, Tris will flip her shit. Is that Damascus steel?"

Chloe, who had no clue what Damascus steel was, pouted because it definitely wasn't hot chocolate.

She had to admit, she was reassured. Comforted in the knowledge that she could still desire some fluffy cocoa with rum rather than just blood, and blood, and more blood, as she'd feared.

She had to ask Levi how the whole drinking blood thing was supposed to work.

She had to ask Levi so many questions. After she was done yelling at him for hiding all this. And snapping her neck. And everything.

"Wootz steel, actually. Faint distinction in the pattern—it's hard to tell at first glance."

Chloe turned on her heel, and there he was. Blood up to his elbow, his suit torn, but he looked so very calm one would have thought he'd just come out of a long, relaxing bath.

"I keep the interesting artifacts under key, though, if you're curious."

Bat scratched his head. "Sorry, mate. We weren't snooping, we were looking for the kitchen."

"Ah, yes. This way."

Chloe remained in the armory, forcing herself to stay put.

Her desire for hot chocolate was long gone. Right now, she didn't need to ask any questions about blood-lust. She needed to bring her teeth to his vein and plunge them in deep.

He smelled of sweat and blood. She'd never encountered such a delicious combination. And the fact that it was delicious was screwing with her head.

She saw him glance at her before exiting the armory with Bat, Gwen, and Blair. And the asshole smiled, as if he knew just what she was going through.

He probably did.

Damn him.

Chloe's mind was easier to distract now than before her change. She looked at the weapons. Every now and then, she'd take one and twirl it around. She had no clue how to use them.

Muscle memory will help. More than you know. It's a wondrous thing. One day, you'll wake up and know all these moves. You'll know how to block, fight, lunge faster. You'll be able to anticipate your adversary's next move with just one hint.

Had he told her that just a week ago? Levi knew

273

exactly what he was doing. The moves she'd learned over the last week had come to her naturally after her change. They were second nature, as if she'd practiced them all her life. But she'd never learned anything about weapons, so she'd have to do that from scratch.

Part of her wished she'd taken up fighting when she'd first arrived at the Institute.

"No hot chocolate for you, then?"

He was back.

Dominion

L evi shut the door behind him. The gentle click of the lock sounded like thunder in the silent weapons hall.

He brought his attention to the volatile newborn vampire who was glaring like she wanted a piece of him.

First things first. "Do you want a report on today's events before we discuss the rest?"

Her jaw was tight. "Would you give me a full report if I asked?"

Fair. He deserved that. "I see no point in deception now. You're considerably more durable."

Still glowering, she nodded.

"The casualties are two huntsmen—one, now that you've healed Bash." He frowned, still confused. "Did I hear that your blood was the cure?"

Chloe nodded. "Eirikr told me our blood was differ-ent, as his—my—family has drunk vampire blood for generations."

Fascinating.

She'd talked to Eirikr himself. He'd guessed as much,

because she was standing, and in one piece; as Tom was in India, based on his last phone call, he'd gleaned she'd somehow convinced their volatile ancestor to help her.

Levi was acutely curious about the other elder, but he was practically salivating to ask for a few drops of her blood to study—and synthesize. But he had a feeling that request wouldn't be well received at the moment. She had questions of her own, and many reasons to be furious with him.

His deception.

His killing her.

"What about the other huntsman?" she asked. "You said two casualties."

Levi watched her closely. New vampires weren't equipped to deal with their newfound strength. Her rage might destroy the whole house.

Never mind. He could build another one.

"He died. I believe he was called Reiss."

Choe gasped and leaned against the glass display case behind her.

Good. She was sad and shocked, but not wrathful. An acquaintance, perhaps a friend, but not a close one.

He kept going. "All ferals were destroyed, and we estimate that about thirty-four vampires escaped Oldcrest's borders. As we've killed another forty, I'd say we haven't heard the last of them. Besides, we found no leader among the bodies we've assembled. Strictly foot soldiers."

Better she focused on the oncoming threat than grief.

He was right to start with that; some of her ire and sorrow disappeared, morphing into concern.

"Do we know more about their queen?"

"Not as of yet, but I'll send orders shortly. Most of my forces will be looking into it. I've also contacted your brother. He's on his way."

Her eyes widened.

"How do you know my brother?" she asked.

Thus prompted, Levi told her everything. His journey to London many moons ago, suspecting what she was at first glance, Tom and Viola's visit, his decision to have her protected while they figured out the real enemy.

"I never expected them to breach Oldcrest. The implication isn't something anyone would like to believe. Someone here has betrayed us. We knew there was a traitor among your entourage because of the scarf. Now we're sure he or she lives here. No one may enter or even find this hill unless they've been invited by a resident. Today's attack wasn't part of the plan. Your brother and I agreed that we wanted you to finish school. Finish learning about our kind, and then ideally start to suspect what you were so the truth might not have been that much of a shock."

He hated the way she'd been turned, surrounded by violence and fear. A born vampire joining their ranks was a joyous event. In the old days, it would have been celebrated.

"Besides, knowing your nature, and speaking of it outside these wards, might have increased the danger to you. We..."

The blow didn't surprise him when it came. She was a lot more collected than most newborns he'd encountered, but he'd known the anger would win eventually.

As well as the lust for his blood. His flesh, his essence.

This, she probably didn't understand.

The shove on his chest was so strong Levi was flung backward, and then she had him pinned on the wall. He could have pushed her back, but what was the point? He rather liked her on top.

"Didn't it occur to you that I might have known there was something wrong with me long before I even got here?" she growled.

"Sure. No doubt you thought you might have ADHD or be bipolar. I doubt you were prepared to hear that you might be a vampire."

She cut him off. "Never again. You will never lie to me."

Levi didn't like making promises he might have to break. If it was in her best interest, if telling her the truth might put her in danger...

She stepped forward, closing the small distance between them, her chest against his.

"Never again," she repeated slowly, weight on every word.

Dammit.

"All right. Never again. I do reserve the right to hide Christmas presents and..."

He never finished the sentence, because her lips were crashing against his.

He smiled under her mouth, his hands pulling her hips closer, pressing her against him. Chloe tasted of forest, wood, and fire. Spices mixed with everything he loved and feared. He couldn't imagine he'd ever get enough. Her mouth left his lips and dropped along his chin, then to his throat, his collarbone. Her fangs grazed his skin, never breaking it. He expected to find her confused by her own craving, but her eyes weren't asking for explanations; they were asking for permission.

"Biting me isn't simple, Chloe. There's something between us—this would only make it stronger."

Unbreakable.

As he'd promised not to lie just moments ago, he knew he had to tell her.

"You're mine. Whatever gods still watch over us occasionally bless our kind with a soul bound to us in a way that's past natural. Taking my blood is a step toward..."

"You talk too much."

Her fangs sank into his shoulder. Levi fell to the ground, not even attempting to still himself as she climbed on top of him and sucked. He threw his head back and moaned, trembling under her mouth, tongue, and fingers. She fumbled with the top of his shirt.

Levi laughed, grabbing both sides of the fabric and ripping it off his torso. He wanted to feel more of her everywhere.

And she obliged. Her mouth lowered to his pecs, nipple, and along his stomach, kissing her way down. He growled, flipping her around so that she was the one seated on the floor, and then he hovered over her, encircling her with his arms.

Two thousand years he'd lived, and in all that time, no one had ever brought him quite so close to madness.

"You got me. What are you going to do with me now?" she questioned.

"Everything."

He started at her earlobe, nibbling it, while his thumb flickered at the apex of her thighs, teasing her heat through layers of fabric. As a human, she should have felt it. Now that she'd turned, he knew it was pure torture, as intense as if he'd directly touched the sensitive flesh of her clit, and yet not quite enough.

"More," she demanded, her breath hot on his skin.

Who was he to refuse her?

He loved savoring her every move and gasp as he took his time with her tank top, lowering the strap on one side and kissing her shoulder, then her stomach, and finally wrapping his mouth around her breast.

"Levi!"

He smiled, sucking at her left nipple and playing with the right. His free hand dipped to her crotch and opened the top button of her muddy jeans before sliding under the fabric. She arched to him when he played her hot inner folds and circled her clit, then pressed on it.

She was so fucking wet, gorgeous, perfect. His.

A younger, less experienced immortal would have bitten her right then. Claimed her body and soul after they exchanged blood. Made her swear herself to him. But she was twenty-five, and they'd known each other three months. What they had was already too soon. Her marking him without understanding what that meant was enough of a shaky beginning. If he rushed this now, he'd regret it until the end of time.

They'd get to know each other. And she'd understand what she was getting herself into when they completed the binding sequence.

For now.

Levi peeled off her pants and flipped her over onto her hands and knees. She pushed her pear-shaped ass up in the air.

Fuck. She looked perfect. Freeing his erection, Levi rubbed it along her wet slit, hitting her clit.

"If you keep teasing me, I swear to God..."

The last word ended in a half-whimper, half-plea as he pushed his length deep inside her tight pussy. Fuck.

He'd had a lot of sex in his day. He hoped they never got around to divulging number of previous partners, because he'd honestly lost count. If he'd had sex with one person a year since his boyhood, the number would have reached four digits. But most years, he'd had more than one woman—and man. A lot more.

He knew the feeling around his cock, his groin, his legs. He'd never felt it in his mind, heart, soul. He wasn't in control. His beast wasn't in control. Something else moved him, making him pound harder, faster, as if to attempt to climb deep beneath her skin and root himself within.

Anchoring her hands on the wall for support, Chloe was meeting him at every thrust, demanding he go deeper, harder. Every part of him was tense, hovering painfully at the top of a cliff, until she tightened around him, her release making him join her in ecstasy.

They were panting like they'd run a thousand miles, his cock still deep inside her.

Levi ran his hand down her back and kissed her delightful ass before finally mentioning, "You know your friends are still here, by the way?"

A New Beginning

Chloe was still cursing Levi. There was no way—none whatsoever—that Blair, Gwen, and the others hadn't heard her yelling like a banshee. He could have mentioned their presence earlier, damn him.

Bat wasn't meeting her eyes, and the witches looked like they were moments from exploding into laughter every time they glanced at her.

Only Tris didn't seem bothered. She was more interested by Chloe's tale.

"And you had no idea you were a fledgling, all along?"

She shrugged. "I mean, I knew I was weird, but no."

Tris glared at Levi. "You should have prepared her better for this."

Part of Chloe felt like she should come to his defense, explain why he hadn't. But she ended up sticking out her tongue at him.

"What she said."

He shrugged, indifferent to the critique.

"It worked out in the end, that's all that matters.

Now, my most immediate concern is the matter of blood. Matters, I should say. You might not be able to survive on typical synthetic human blood."

Oh. Good point. Eirikr had said that their family drank vampire blood; did that make it their exclusive food source?

But no. Eirikr himself had survived for so long on whatever he could find.

"Maybe I could adapt," she said, hopeful.

Levi shook his head. "No reason to. We just need to get working on vampire synthetic blood."

Chloe opened her mouth to protest, then closed it again when the implication of that hit her.

Let him work on it if he wanted. She could think of a way to use it.

"There's something else I wanted to talk to you about," Levi said. "With your authorization, I would like to analyze your blood. The ferals bite several vampires every year. With luck, I'll be able to synthesize a cure from whatever antigen courses in your system. As the elusive queen has found a way to control the ferals, reversing their contamination is more important than ever."

Tris added, "And you'll be able to help the ferals you keep locked up for observation."

What was that?

"You have people locked up?" she asked, incredulous.

Levi inclined his head. "They're killed on sight when vampires encounter them. I spare them and try to treat them. Unsuccessfully, for the last hundreds of years, but..."

"And we were playing hot dog in a roll while there are people locked up that I could help?"

She was stunned.

Levi stiffened.

"Chloe, Bash was in transition toward feral. There may be no aiding those who were bitten weeks or months ago."

"Don't you think," she replied tightly, "that we at least ought to try?"

He hesitated. "I hoped you'd feel that way. But I wouldn't have presumed to ask you to bleed..."

She rolled her eyes. "I'm a woman. I bleed every month. Come on. Let's go."

The galleries underneath the Institute were more dungeon than lab, but they'd been fitted with the latest technology. Chloe didn't need to go anywhere near the crazed vampires. Levi took vials of her blood to his office and distributed it to the cells remotely.

The creatures devoured it gruesomely.

All but a little boy quietly sitting on his bed, sipping at the vial, and commenting, "It tastes better than usual. Seasoning?"

"That's Steven. He's been here for months. He's my unexplainable factor. He was infected—we have records and video showing it. But by the time he came to me, he was...like this. Fine. His blood tests still show signs of infection, but it's not affecting him."

Suddenly taken by an idea, Chloe pressed the intercom Levi had used earlier to greet the subjects.

"Hey. Steven, right?"

"That's my name. I don't know your name. I don't know you at all."

He sounded a little off, but so would anyone after spending so long in a cage.

"I'm Chloe. Can I ask you a question, Steven?"

"You just did. Feel free to ask a second. I'm bored."

"Where are you from?" she asked.

He blinked, as if trying to remember.

"New Jersey."

So much for that.

Understanding her train of thoughts, Levi pressed the button again. "Where were you when you started feeling better, Steven? Do you remember?"

He tilted his head.

"I was...somewhere in Colorado. Can't remember where. I'd just drunk from a man. Human, I think. He tasted good, too. Seasoned."

Chloe gasped. "That's where I'm from," she told Levi. "I bet that was my brother, or father, or, I don't know, one of our ancestors."

Levi was frantically taking notes, grinning all the way.

Then they waited. And waited. And waited some more.

Hours passed, then days.

On Tuesday morning, Chloe left for a few hours to attend Reiss's funeral in the meadow behind the Institute. All of Coscnoc was gathered in reverential silence. Then, when the witches began to sing, all joined in. Chloe didn't know the lyrics, but she sang anyway, humming along to the ageless tune of farewell.

For the first time since Sunday night, as the wind picked up and she felt her friends shiver around her, she realized something.

She wasn't cold.

Gwen and Blair accompanied her back to the dorms and helped her pack her bags.

"Are you sure this is necessary?" Gwen asked.

Blair nodded. "Newborns are volatile. And besides, it's the same house."

She was moving to the right-hand side of the dorm, with the rest of the dangerous students.

Including Tris and Jack.

Her new room was five times the size of the old one and ten times more luxurious.

"Same walls?" Blair asked.

Chloe shook her head. She'd changed too much to cling to the past.

"What color, then?"

"You pegged me well in January. Do it again."

Her mentor tilted her head, thinking for a moment. Then she repeated her spell. This time, the walls were dark purple, and the flowers gold.

BETWEEN FORTY AND SEVENTY-THREE HOURS AFTER drinking her blood, each subject in the containment levels woke up disorientated, confused, and angry.

All were cured.

Chloe would have given whatever drops of blood she could spare to help, but Levi didn't let her. He and the alchemist, Alexius, removed some of her marrow and started to work on a synthetic remedy instead.

He was busy, and so was she, catching up on days of work and a project that wasn't easy to organize from Oldcrest. Delivery companies didn't actually pop by the shielded sup territory. But she bribed Tris to pick up some stuff in the nearby towns.

The next Friday, her project was ready.

Chloe gathered the boxes she'd ordered during the week and set off.

When her eyes caught a silhouette she hadn't talked to since that dreadful day on the hill, she changed course.

She rushed to the lake behind the three hills, biting her lip.

Claim

The blond man in the white suit noticed her approaching. She could tell from the way he stiffened but didn't turn to greet her.

Shit.

"I'm sorry, Jack, about Reiss and Bash."

She never had the chance to speak to him after the funeral.

He shrugged, throwing a stone that ricocheted off the surface of the water.

"It sucks about Reiss," he admitted. "But he knew what he was getting into. Just because we're catching a break behind these walls doesn't change what it means to be huntsmen. We protect the world from darkness. And yes, we get hurt doing so. Nothing new. He'll be honored as any warrior."

Chloe hated every single word he'd just said. She hated that this world existed, that it was normal to lose a twenty-eight-year-old to a pack of monsters.

"As for Bash," he added, "what are you sorry for exactly?"

She felt like it was a trick question, but she answered anyway.

"He died."

Jack had turned to her now. "So did you," he replied quietly.

Chloe's heart skipped a beat.

She had died. She remembered the sound of her snapping neck echoing in her ears. The girl she'd been, her mortal shell, had ceased to exist. And yet she felt no loss, no attachment to that person.

"I evolved, Jack. I may not have known it, but I was always meant to be this. I've never felt more like myself. My mind, scattered as it is, is finally entirely mine. I found myself. Bash lost who he was."

Words came easier to her now, too. Everything made sense. Her own brain, her strange desires. Even her father's descent into insanity.

She would not have Jack, or anyone else, feel sorry for her now.

Jack nodded. "I'm not sure how to help him now. How to guide him. Tris will turn eventually, but it's different. She's learned to be both a huntsman and a vampire her entire life. Bash..."

Again, she knew what to say.

"Be his friend. That voice at the other end of the phone if he ever calls. But not his boss. If he chooses to be a hunter after he accepts his nature, you'll be the first to know. For now, he's one of us. Trying to accept himself like this is going to take time."

Bash was staying in Levi's house, and each time she'd visited, he'd been in that very study where she'd given him her blood, on that sofa. Reading. Sleeping. Maybe just avoiding her eyes.

Jack watched her intensely.

"Are you claiming him?"

The word had meaning, she could tell, and she didn't want to make promises she couldn't keep. She tilted her head.

"Are you claiming him as part of your clan, your family? Do you swear you'll take care of him?"

Maybe the old Chloe wasn't quite gone yet. Part of her was terrified at the prospect of being responsible for anyone at all, let alone a brand-new vampire, when she didn't even understand herself what it entailed.

But she wasn't just a newly risen vamp. She was an Eirikrson. The head of the Eirikrsons, as long as their forefather remained stuck in his cave.

Chloe had learned in Immortal History that most vampires no longer had any affiliation—they just lived their lives as they saw fit. But in the old days, almost everyone was sworn to one of the seven houses.

"I'll claim him if he wants to belong to my house," she said. Knowing that Jack was after more than idle words, Chloe added, "I swear it."

He relaxed a little.

"Where were you going with all that?"

She looked down at the boxes in her arms. Heavy as they were, she hadn't noticed them for the last few minutes.

"Oh."

She blushed, ashamed to spell it out. No doubt Jack would think she was crazy.

"I..." She cleared her throat. "I owe someone."

Jack smiled. "Better settle that debt, then. In our world, debts are as dangerous as oaths and curses."

On her way up to Coscnoc, Chloe was annoyed at

herself. She'd lied. No debt was leading her feet up the familiar hill and down the long dark path.

When she arrived at the door, she had to walk sideways to fit through it with the cardboard boxes. Finally, she reached the cave under the hill.

Eirikr was sitting on the ground. He looked thinner, far less lively. And surprised. Mostly surprised.

"You're back."

She dropped the three boxes.

"I hope you're handy with a screwdriver? The bed comes in pieces. I'll bring the mattress in a sec. Levi offered to carry it, but I figured you might eat him, so I made him stay behind."

His sharp eyes remained on her, calculating. Trying to see what she wanted from him, she guessed.

She sighed.

"All right, so I'm actually pretty short on family members, and you look cool. Plus, this place really needs decorating. Are you more of a purple or a green guy, by the way?"

Eirikr blinked.

"You are back," he repeated—just a quiet whisper.

Then she understood. He'd doubted her existence at first, suspecting she was an illusion. A fantasy.

She wondered how many times he'd dreamed of this. Not her, specifically, but someone, anyone, coming down here for a chat. There was nothing in this cave. Nothing at all. He'd been entirely forsaken for centuries.

Regardless of what he might have done, he didn't deserve that. No one did.

"If you could get out of here," she said, "what would you do?"

Eirikr had never lied to her, and although he might have then, he chose not to.

"Destroy the world as you know it. Probably. Although I definitely want to try Starbucks first."

She sighed.

"Fortunately, it's not a matter you'll need to concern yourself with anytime soon, little daughter. I cannot get out of here. Only the witch who cast me out in the first place can undo this spell, and she's long returned to dust."

Chloe nodded and opened the smallest and most important of her three boxes. She couldn't get him out of here, but she could make his life a little more comfortable. She pulled out a bag of synthesized vampire blood.

"I know. Not quite Starbucks."

Eirikr was speechless for a beat, but he wasn't one to remain so for long.

He smirked and reached out for the bag.

"It'll do."

She didn't so much as turn to check who'd entered her room when she heard the door open behind her. As if she could mistake *him*. His presence. His scent.

Chloe's eyes remained on her reflection. She looked the same, more or less. Except for the eyes. Sometimes they were dark brown, as they used to be.

Other times, when her throat tightened in hunger, and her fangs popped out...she was someone else entirely. Someone with bright blue eyes and a heart of stone.

"You're sure you want to stay here?"

She giggled. The sound was utterly unfamiliar. Someone's voice. A soprano, too suave and seductive.

"So, what, we date for a few weeks and you want me to move in?"

Levi chuckled, wrapped his arms around her waist. "Yes," he whispered against her throat. "I very much want you in my house, chained to my bed twenty-four seven."

His mouth touched her collarbone, and kiss their way up to her jaw. She bit her lower lip hard enough to draw blood.

"But I meant, you could move into your home. Skyhall."

Her home. The black palace at the very top of the hill. She hadn't stepped inside yet.

Chloe shook her head.

"We've made a statement already. The world knows what I am. They know the Eirikrson are back."

And she didn't mind that, strangely. She wanted the arrogant, heartless immortals who played with lives casually to be afraid.

"But I'm also Chloe Miller. Barely trained. With no understanding of my powers or my limits. And no control over my thirst."

She drank from Levi's throat, and from the countless bags of synthetic blood he made available to her everywhere. But she was hungry. Thirsty. Always.

"Moving onto to hill will say to the world that I'm ready. That I've claimed my house. And that they can come knocking if they want to challenge me. I don't think I can do that yet."

Levi pulled her in closer.

"Not yet," he agreed. "But soon."

The End
Next in After Darkness Falls: *Blood of a Huntsman*.

May Sage juggles multiple series and prioritizes those which are well reviewed. If you want to speed up the releases in the After Darkness Falls series, don't forget to leave a review!

T *wo thousand years ago*

THE CREATURE OBSERVED THE WITCH FROM THE darkness without a single word, its penetrating gaze as bright as a star in the darkness. A weaker witch might have fallen for it.

"I'm not afraid of you," Aurora lied. "You cannot reach me." This was said with a little more conviction. "I may not be able to kill you, but these walls will be your tomb."

"How poetic. And these markings..." His hands touched the stone on either side of the open doorway she'd spelled. "They're positively artful. Tatiana evidently didn't waste her aureus when she sent you to study the ways of the great wizards of Alexandria. But you're smarter than this, Rora."

"Don't call me that," she spat.

She'd fallen for it once. His beauty, his harsh and melodious voice. His spells.

He was dangerous, to her and to the rest of her kind. To all humanity. She was doing the right thing. For once in her life, she'd made the right decision.

"Fine. Aurora, then. You don't want to do this. These walls will never keep me. We both know it. You're doing nothing except delaying the inevitable."

"I am protecting my race from a monster," Aurora yelled.

She'd seen what he'd done. The hundreds of bodies, defiled, drained. Finally, she saw him for what he was.

"You're doing a coward's dirty work and turning your back on the only person who's ever been on your side," said Eirikr Primus, bastard of Markus Aurelius.

The first of his name, the first of his kind.

Not the last.

Hundreds of vampires now roamed the lands. She'd find them, too. This wouldn't end until they were all ashes.

"I don't want to see you waste your life on a fruitless endeavor. Let me go. I won't hurt you. I will never hurt you or let any of mine lay a finger on you. You know this."

She'd never doubted it. Even now, she was certain that the monster wouldn't harm her.

But his gentleness wasn't about her. Aurora looked remarkably like her grandmother, which she knew was the only reason she hadn't been drained of blood the moment they'd met.

"Trust me, Rora."

Aurora straightened her spine.

"You will remain here, in the company of the only thing you've ever loved—yourself. Rot in hell."

She turned her heels, heading up the stairs that led out into the sunlight.

❦

THREE MONTHS AGO

EIRIKR REMEMBERED THE SMELL OVERHEAD. NOT THE stench as it was now, full of toxic fumes and rotting flesh. Even in his prison, so dark and deep he couldn't see the light of day, he smelled the new air. The last two thousand years had not suited their dear Earth.

But he remembered still. Watching the flocks of sheep from a mountaintop, and breathing so deeply, taking it for granted.

They hadn't been his sheep. Nothing, by rights, had ever been his.

Eirikr was a bastard, born of a Roman scum based in Raetia, meaning he owned none of his mother's property and certainly none of the man who'd fathered him. He'd believed his fate had been watching over his little brother's folks. It could have been worse. They weren't poor, and there was food on the table every night.

Then, one day, the Roman came; the one who looked like him.

"Are you the one they call bastard, boy?"

He understood enough of their foreign tongue to nod.

"We're to return to Rome. You look well enough. Come with me if you wish."

Until then, no one had asked about his wishes. Eirikr followed, and was named Primerius, the first natural son of Markus Aurelius, a famed general.

The man did not value weakness, so Eirikr trained every morning, every evening, often through the night, until he was known as one of the best soldiers in his regiment. He learned to desire many things, though none as much as the beautiful Tatiana, priestess of Pompeii. They said she was a daughter of Zeus, and no one who looked upon her doubted it. But she gave her favor to him, a bastard, against all odds.

When she was called to banish the monster who'd taken residence in Pompeii and dismembered so many souls, drinking the blood of her victims, Eirikr volunteered to protect her.

Tatiana was so beautiful, and nature seemed to bend to her will. Eirikr never doubted she'd win. She could win against any enemy, any monster, any demon sent from the belly of the Earth.

But the moment they entered the creature's lair, he knew how mistaken he was.

The enemy was fast as a shadow, brutal as the waves crashing against the cliffs, and so striking she outshone even Tatiana, when she stopped long enough for them to see more than a blur.

She killed two dozen guards in mere instants and then moved against Tatiana herself. Eirikr didn't know what made him move, his broken body so weak, writhing on the floor, but he caught her shapely shin and bit, deep, desperate to hurt her, to distract her long enough to give his love time to run.

The monster's skin was like stone, hard marble, but Eirikr's teeth were sharp, and though it hurt, he bit hard enough to draw blood. Golden blood, luminous in the darkness.

Tatiana had an instant to run. Eirikr was kicked in the face so hard his neck broke.

That evening, he rose.

The creature was still here, in the darkness, weeping over the corpses, demanding to know why she couldn't stop herself from killing, why she was still alive, why she was so very alone.

When he stirred, she rose, gasped, and rushed to him.

"Impossible," she mouthed, her voice so melodious Eirikr almost forgot he hated everything she was.

Almost.

Her fingers were gentle as she explored all his wounds, now closed.

"You were dead. You should be dead."

He felt dead. Everything inside him hurt. He could barely move. His brain pulsed with one need, one desire.

The gold blood in her veins.

"How!" she demanded to know.

He wasn't sure he heard, but he said the only word that would cross his lips.

"*Sangui*—"

Speaking hurt his throat, so very dry he felt like he'd never drunk a drop of water. Water would not quench this thirst. Nothing would.

The creature lifted her arm to her sharp teeth and bit down before presenting it to him. His mouth closed on the gash and he drank, sealing his fate.

His vision cleared. His aching limbs had never felt better. He was alive. He was reborn in the image of the monster who'd destroyed him.

The creature was ecstatic, overjoyed. She felt better. Her need to kill had passed. She spoke of the future, a future where she didn't destroy city after city, because she'd have him, and many like him, at her side.

Eirikr laughed. He laughed so hard.

"I will destroy you. I will destroy everything you cherish. You're a demon, and this earth will not have peace while you walk among us."

For a time, he did just that.

For a time. And then, when he was no longer able to, his descendants did so on his behalf. They'd changed with the time. They no longer had to hunt all of Ariadne's creatures, as some had ceased to represent a threat to the world. Eirikr had little patience for their weakness. He was irritated, frustrated to be stuck in his prison.

For fifteen hundred years, he was displeased. Then came the betrayal he should have foreseen. His kind banded together and destroyed all of his children, and his children's children.

And then he knew despair. He'd never understood that this was his fate, his end. That he'd never again smell the air. That he'd never fulfill his vow. Until now. He had no one on Earth, no one to help him, no one to care if he turned into dust. His nights were long and dark. Many a time, he wished for an end, for a death that wouldn't come, even when he was parched and decaying. He was the first of the ancients, and therefore, the most powerful. Ariadne hadn't understood the process yet. She gave him so much of the divine blood running through her veins that she turned him into her equal. A mistake she never repeated.

Eirikr had stopped counting the days centuries ago.

He didn't feel the wind or rain. He ignored the small rodents who walked by him as if he was nothing but stone. He was stone.

Until...

"What's down there?"

The voice cut through his mind's fog like thunder in a cloudy sky. Then came a burst of wind carrying a scent he recognized. His.

"Nothing you should concern yourself with," someone told his daughter.

In the darkness of his prison, Eirikr lifted his head half an inch.

A squirrel walked by, unsuspecting. Too long had passed since creatures had been murdered in this cave for the squirrel to think better of it. Swift as shadow, Eirikr wrapped his hands around it and broke its neck. He brought it to his lips and drank it dry.

⸙

"LOVE THE HAIR, BY THE WAY," SAID ONE OF THE girls. "Good luck getting an ombre like that in town, though."

Chloe laughed. "That won't be a problem," she said, pointing to her head. "Natural color."

"Cool," Natalie told her.

The creature watching at the edge of the Wolvs-woods narrowed his eyes and then broke into a run, heading up Night Hill.

"What is she?" Mikar demanded.

It wasn't in his character to demand anything of his liege. He'd served Levi for three hundred years, since the elder had turned him, and in all this time, he'd never questioned one of his orders.

Because until now, they'd made sense.

"You call me back from a sensitive mission in Russia to babysit a regular? Fine. Your prerogative. You're the boss. But now she outruns a killing machine and has magic fucking hair?"

Levi had entirely ignored him until then, writing at his desk, but this made him lift his head and smile.

"Magic hair?"

"Black, then silver. I don't know, man. She's definitely not normal."

"Do you think I would have recalled my right hand, along with my closest acquaintance, for the sake of someone *normal?*" Levi asked pointedly.

He wasn't going to say anything, was he?

"I don't get it. Just tell me this is important. It's not fun, Lev. I like killing and fucking and dancing. I can't do any of that here."

"It's important," Levi echoed before returning to his writing without another word.

Jeez. As ancient, all-powerful, noble vampires went, Levi wasn't that bad, normally, but the man obviously could be a dick.

"Tell me I don't need to enroll in the Institute."

"You need to do three things, and only three. I've already informed you of your duties; I will not repeat them."

He had. The day Levi had visited him in Moscow, he'd said he needed Mikar to watch a girl.

"Make sure she doesn't get decapitated, drowned, or burned. That's all I ask of you."

At the time, Mikar had translated that to "ensure no one kills her." Now he understood his mistake.

Mikar stilled, comprehension finally hitting him.

Levi didn't care at all about Chloe getting killed. What mattered was *how*.

"Oh."

Well, that certainly changed things.

"Yes, *oh*. Now, you better get back to work."

Mikar did as he was told, no further complaint crossing his lips.

"You've got to talk to the girl."

Levi lifted his eyes to his foreman, surprised and rather vexed. It wasn't like Mikar to question his orders at all, and he'd done it twice in as many weeks.

"You and I both know the walls, woods, and waters in Coscnoc have ears. I can't afford to."

Mikar's jaw was set. "I don't get it. What's the big deal if the conclave hears..."

"Don't. Don't speak. Don't bring attention to what you're doing."

His house was safe enough to discuss most of his business, but he wouldn't talk of Chloe out loud anywhere.

Levi was as frustrated as his second. Not being able to give him the information he needed was inconvenient, but he couldn't take the risk.

Those who were moving against Chloe were weak. They were also careful, disguising each step and hiring pawns, but they were failing because their effort was pathetic. But that would change once the world knew what Levi had gathered the moment he'd seen her.

"Listen to me, Levi. I won't be able to keep things to myself if she keeps pushing. She's a whisper."

Levi got up from his desk and faced the window, looking down the hill toward Adairford.

A whisper.

He hadn't spent enough time with her to know much about her, but it made sense from what he'd seen—from what he knew. She'd been nothing but a waitress to Charles and Michelle White, but the two power-hungry leaders had stopped their machinations for long enough to protect her. And there was also the way she'd gotten under his skin so easily, with a few well-placed words. She'd known exactly what to say to him.

Whispers were the sirens of vampires, magnetic and charming to a degree that was dangerous. They could get anything handed to them on a silver platter if they just batted their eyelids and asked. In mortal fledglings, that translated to highly popular individuals who rarely made enemies. They were often protected, cared for.

Chloe had always been precious; all born vampires were. He hadn't realized she was also a valuable asset.

Levi's fingers hammered impatiently against the closest wall.

He'd told her the truth about wanting to snap her neck. She was old enough to turn. He stopped himself only because she had no idea what she was yet. Fledglings were prepared their entire lives for the change. They knew what came before, during, and after. She didn't. In a perfect world, he could just tell her, show her the skills she had to gain before her transition. But the moment those words crossed his lips, the six most powerful families in this world would set aside all conflict and team up to destroy her before she became their greatest fear.

Five centuries had passed since a member of the seventh founding family had turned. Anyone else would have thought it was impossible. They would have thought that she was just an obscure descendant from one of the other six, somehow lost in their careful records. They'd wiped out her entire line, for good reason.

But Levi remembered the day they'd come for the last survivors, here on this very hill. He'd been in his home when he'd heard the commotion; however, he knew one thing no one else did. There had been a little boy, three years old, who was fond of swimming in the lake. His nurse had taken him outside that morning, and as every member of his family was torn apart, he swam in blissful oblivion.

Levi could have ended everything. Instead, he took the child and dropped him in front of a church.

Drowning the boy would have been smarter for many reasons, but Levi couldn't bring himself to do it.

Five hundred years without any sign, any news. He'd believed the line had died out, until he saw her, the spitting image of her forefathers down to that hair. Dark at the roots, blonde after an inch. When she turned, it would be silver.

Levi did his homework after she emerged, researching her family. The trail of bodies following her line was subtle but staggering. No wonder. The longer a born vampire took to turn, the more bloodthirsty and brutal they became. Levi had waited until he was thirty-two, and it had been a push. Her family tree wasn't complete, but wherever he could trace it, he found inexplicable, ritualistic murders. Chloe's father, at forty-nine, was a murderer and a cannibal because he had needs he hadn't understood—the need for blood and the hunt. The needs of a vampire in the body of a mortal. No doubt most of her ancestors who'd reached that age had also lost their minds. The only difference was that they hadn't been caught.

She was an Eirikrson.

They were monsters. Vampires who only drank vampire blood. The head of their family had created the huntsmen to hunt down and murder any vampire—not just the rogues, at the beginning. When she turned, she'd be just like them, the nightmare they whispered about in the dark.

The reasonable thing would be to destroy her before she could obliterate hundreds of years of peace. She wasn't a little boy Levi couldn't bring himself to murder. He should have beheaded her in London. He should have ordered Mikar to burn her alive, if he was too squeamish to do it himself. But he couldn't, because fate was a bitch. Like it or not, he was on the girl's side.

If you enjoyed After Darkness Falls...

EXCERPT FROM DEAD OF NIGHT BY EMILY
GOODWIN—COPYRIGHT 2019

Lucas's gaze meets my eyes, and I swear if his heart could beat, it would hammer right along with mine. The night stands still around us, and the busy city fades. All I can see is Lucas standing in front of me, looking at me with so much lust in his eyes it's making me feel like I caught him in the act. Or rather...that he caught me in the act.

"Your heart is beating faster." His fingers are barely touching the flesh on my neck, in the slope where it meets my shoulder.

"Yeah, it does that sometimes."

He steps in, bringing his other hand to the hem of my dress. Slowly, he bunches it up and slides his hand along my thigh. My eyes fall shut and I rest my hands on his hips so he can't see them shaking.

Inhaling deep, he presses his fingers into the flesh on the back of my thigh. Moving his other hand back up my neck, he pushes it into my hair and brings my head back a bit, exposing my neck to him.

The wind picks up, blowing my hair around us. I

open my eyes to see Lucas's lips pull back a bit as he draws his fangs.

"You," he starts and puts his lips to my neck, gently kissing my skin. A shiver runs through me and my knees threaten to buckle. "Are." He kisses me again. "Beautiful." He pulls his lips back, letting his fangs graze along my skin. His hand is already in my hair. He could force me back and drink my blood, draining enough to weaken me in just seconds.

And enough to kill me in less than a minute.

He trails kisses down my neck and over my shoulder, pushing the thin strap of my dress out of the way. I tighten my hold on him, afraid of falling if I let go. My eyes flutter shut again, and he presses his fangs down, harder than before but not enough to break the skin. I gasp, thinking he's going to bite me.

Because I'm going to let him.

I want him to.

To have me.

Taste me.

But he doesn't bite me, and instead kisses and sucks the spot on my neck that sends an instant wave of heat through me. I whimper as he rakes his hand through my hair, bringing his other hand up my thigh and under my dress until it rests on the base of my ass.

"You didn't agree with me," he says and his deep voice rattles right through me.

"I didn't...what?"

"You are exquisite. You're powerful. You're beautiful. You...you've surprised me more in the few days I've known you than others have in their entire lifetimes."

I sink my teeth into my bottom lip, trying to keep it from quivering. I'm feeling everything right now. Turned on. Vulnerable. I want to break down and confess everything I've repressed. I want to cry about my past, curse everyone who's hurt me, and tell him about every single heartbreak. And at the same time, I don't want to say a word. I want him to lay me down on the lounge chair behind us and fuck me hard, making it impossible to feel anything other than the pleasure his big cock brings me.

"Lucas," I start, but never get to finish. He puts his lips to mine and the heat rushing through me explodes, sending tingles of desire to every nerve in my body. Opening my mouth, I deepen the kiss, wrapping my arms around him.

Bringing his hand down, he grips my ass and pulls me to him. He presses his fangs against my lip just hard enough to send a jolt through me. When he said he was able to control himself, he wasn't kidding. Though I suppose this is what sixteen hundred years of sex will do.

Holy shit.

Lucas has nearly two thousand years of experience. Of perfecting. Of knowing exactly what he likes. Of how to please others. He slides his hand around my leg, going between my thighs. "When I slip my fingers inside your panties, will I find your pussy wet for me?"

I open my mouth, but it takes me a second to gather a coherent thought. Because his words are making me wetter than I already am.

"Why don't you find out?" I pant.

A guttural growl comes from deep inside his throat and he turns me around so that my ass is pressed right up against his cock, feeling it harden. He gathers my hair in one hand and pulls it to the side. I tip my head, arching my neck and offering it to him. He brings his mouth down, kissing and sucking at my skin. His fangs scrape me as he kisses me, and the bit of pain mixed in with the pleasure makes me even hotter. He's hardly touched me and I'm getting so wound up, so turned on I don't know how much longer I can stand it.

Want to read more? Dead of Night is available here.

28059146R00187

Printed in Great Britain
by Amazon